Dedalus European C

General Editor: David

Dedalus / Hippocrene

FOUQUÉ DE LA MOTTE

UNDINE

with an introduction by Ben Barkow
and
illustrations by Rosie M. Pitman

Dedalus / Hippocrene

Published in the UK by Dedalus Ltd,
Langford Lodge, St Judith's Lane, Sawtry, Cambs, PE17 5XE
Published in the USA by Hippocrene Books Inc.,
171 Madison Avenue, New York NY10016

ISBN 0 946626 57 6

First published in Germany in 1811
Dedalus edition 1990

Introduction copyright © Dedalus 1990

Printed in Great Britain by
Richard Clay Ltd, Bungay, Suffolk

A CIP listing for this title is available on request

INTRODUCTION

What we have before us is a German *Märchen*. Not, however, a *Volksmärchen*, an authentic folk story of the kind being assiduously gathered and polished for public consumption by contemporaries such as Jakob and Wilhelm Grimm. Rather, Fouqué's work is a *Kunstmärchen*, a sort of literary pastiche. Works of this type were composed by Goethe (in 1795), Ludwig Tiech, Clemens Brentano and E. T. A. Hoffmann among others. Fouqué's tale is a highly wrought work of art drawing on and appealing to the spirit of *völkisch*-ness resurgent in the Germany of his day.

Friedrich Heinrich Karl de la Motte Fouqué was born on 12 February 1777 in Brandenburg, Prussia. His family were Huguenots, originating in Normandy. They fled to Prussia after the revocation of the Edict of Nantes. He began his career as a soldier, following his father and grand-father (who had been one of Friedrich the Great's generals). After 1803, when he married for the second time, he devoted himself wholeheartedly to literature. Aside from producing an astonishing number of plays, stories, poems, and translations (most of them now disparaged as worthless) he was also active as an editor, both of books and journals. Among his major works the poetic trilogy *Der Held Des Nordens* (The Hero of the North) is noteworthy as the first modern treatment of the Nibelungen saga. These poems greatly influenced and inspired Richard Wagner. *Undine* is universally recognized as his masterpiece.

Fouqué's star rose fast. The Nibelungen poems established him in the public mind as a leading exponent of popular romanticism. *Undine* boosted his reputation to its zenith. Contemporaries saw in him a writer of extraordinary verve and virtuosity. For Goethe, *Undine* was "allerliebst" (best beloved). Heinrich Heine honoured him as unique among epic poets of the day in carrying the public with him. Joseph von Eichendorff acknowledged him as the leading representative of the Romantic school. However, by mid-century his reputation had plummeted. He was seen as embodying the worst of brash nationalism, the crassest sort of *kitsch*. He was accused of having sold his talent for the sake of cheap popularity, and of having had no talent to begin with. Revealingly, some of the most virulent attacks came from those who had been lavish with their praise earlier. Only *Undine* survived this critical onslaught.

Fouqué took his inspiration for *Undine* from a work by the Swiss physician and iatrochemist Paracelsus. He had discovered Paracelsus through the work of Jakob Böhme, a 17th century pantheistic writer, who was enjoying a revival among German Romantics. Böhme directed him towards a work entitled *Liber de nymphis, sylphis, Pygmaeis et Salamandris, et de cafeteria spiritibus* in which he found a discussion of various kinds of water-spirits including nymphs and undines. These latter are there characterised as unique in the spirit world on account of their ability to assume human form. Like all spirits they lack a human soul, but can acquire one if they marry a mortal. However, if their spouse repudiates them on or near water they again lose their hard-won soul and are back to square one.

From this book, then, Fouqué got not only his basic idea but most of his plot as well. He saw in it an opportunity to address some of the fundamental issues of the Romantic movement, such as the primary division between the innocence of nature and the suffering of guilty humanity. It is striking that Undine, in her innocent natural state, while certainly frolicsome, is shallow and unappealing, self-willed and irresponsible. With marriage she undergoes a transformation, deepening into a sensitive, devoted, somewhat sorrowful, literally *soulful* woman. The tragic irony of the tale is that only the entirely human experience of betrayal reveals the extent of her goodness and worth while simultaneously robbing her of the essential human attribute.

Like the bulk of Fouqué's output, *Undine* is set in a historically non-specific but distant past, the golden days of Nordic chivalry and heroism. He was seeking to foster a specifically Germanic sence of nationhood and identity, rooted in a heroic past, with which to oppose the military humiliation and political domination of the German lands by the French. It's worth noting that with the end of the Napoleonic wars Fouqué's popularity waned as the felt need for *völkisch* consolations declined.

Undine was first published in a quarterly journal, *Die Jahreszeiten* (The Seasons) in the Spring issue of 1811. Its success was immediate, and it appeared in book form later that year. By the end of the century it had passed through more than 26 editions at home and been translated into every major European language.

Interestingly, *Undine* was immensely popular in Britain during the last quarter of the 19th century. In 1897 alone, two new translations were published, of which the present is one. Perhaps the tale's lilting idyll offered escape and succour in a world of industrial frightfulness, social terror and, increasingly, *fin de siècle* gloom. Possibly its vision of female nature and destiny was a comfort to those appalled or frightened by feminism, emancipation, the "woman question" (typified perhaps by the shocking sight of velocopedist girls tearing around the countryside flaunting conventions of modesty and seemliness in their near-obscene "bifurcateds", or trousers). Whatever the reason, the book sold like hot cakes, aided no doubt by its appealing low level and innocuous eroticism.

The influence of *Undine* has been lasting. It was made into an opera by E. T. A. Hoffman in 1816 (libuetto by Fouqué), by K. F. Girschner in 1837 and also by G. A. Lortzing in 1845. In addition it was turned into a ballet in 1958 by H. W. Henze (performed in Covent Garden; choreography by Ashton, conducted by Henze, with Fonteyn in the lead). The story formed the basis of *Ondine*, a play by Jean Giraudoux, was used by Hans Christian Anderson for *The Little Mermaid* and by Oscar Wilde in his collection of fairy tales.

Ben Barkow

CHRONOLOGY

1777   Birth of Friedrich Heinrich Karl, Freiherr de la Motte Fouqué in Brandenburg, Prussia on 12 February.

1778/9 Herder publishes his collection of German folk poetry, *Volkslieder*.

1781   Publication of Schiller's play *Die Räuber*. Kant establishes German idealism in philosophy with the publication of his *Critique of Pure Reason* .

1786   Friedrich Wilhelm II comes to the Prussian throne.

1787   Mozart's *Don Giovanni* premiered.

1789   Start of Revolution in France.

1794   Enters the Prussian army and sees active service.

1799   Napoleon Bonaparte comes to power in France as a result of the Revolution of the 18th Brumaire (November 9).

1803   Marries Karoline von Briest, resigns his commision and settles on her estates at Nennhausen, west of Berlin, to devote his time to literature. His first three dramatic works are published, under the pseudonym Pellegrin, by Friedrich von Schlegel in his periodical *Europa*.

1804   August von Schlegel publishes Fouqué's *Dramatische Spiele*, again pseudonymously. Napoleon is crowned Emperor of France.

1805   Napoleon defeats the Austrians at the Battle of Austerlitz on 2 December.

1806   Prussia declares war on France in October and suffers a crushing defeat. Napoleon enters Berlin on 25 October.

1810 Publishes *Der Held Nordens*.

1811 First puplication of **Undine**. Goethe publishes
Dichtung und Wahrheit.

1812 Napoleon invades Russia with the Grand Army and
suffers terrible defeats. The brothers Grimm begin
publication of their collection of German folkstories,
Kinder und Hausmärchen.

1813 Prussia declares war on France on 17 March. Fouqué
joins regiment of volunteers, sees action and serves
with distinction. Napoleon defeated at Leipzig in
Battle of the Nations, 16-19 October, marking the en
of his reign in Germany. Publication of Fouqué's *Der
Zauberring*.

1814 France invaded by Prussia and England. Paris
surrenders on 30 March. Napoleon abdicates on 6
April and retires to Elba.

1815 Napoleon returns to France until defeated at
Waterloo. He is banished to St. Helena. Fouqué
returns to private life and resumes his literary career
Publication of his *Sintram*.

1816 He begins publication of the five-volume collection of
poetry, *Gedichte,* which will continue until 1827.

1821 Death of Napoleon on St. Helena in May.

1831 Fouqué's wife dies. He lectures on modern history and
poetics in Halle.

1842 He is called to Berlin by Friedrich Willhelm II and
given a pension.

1843 Fouqué dies in Berlin on January 23.

HOW THE KNIGHT CAME TO THE FISHERMAN

THE FISHERMAN'S COTTAGE

UNDINE

CHAPTER I

HOW THE KNIGHT CAME TO THE FISHERMAN

HERE was once, it may be now many hundred years ago, a good old fisherman, who was sitting one fine evening before his door, mending his nets. The part of the country in which he lived was extremely pretty. The green sward, on which his cottage stood, ran far into the lake, and it seemed as if it was from love for the blue clear waters that the tongue of land had stretched itself out into them, while with an equally fond embrace the lake had encircled the green pasture rich with waving grass and flowers, and the refreshing shade of trees. The one welcomed the other, and it was just this that made each so beautiful. There were indeed few human beings, or rather none at all, to be met with on this pleasant spot, except the fisherman and his family. For at the back of this little promontory, there lay a very wild forest, which, both from its gloom and pathless solitude as well as from the wonderful creatures and illusions with which it was said to abound, was avoided by most people except in cases of necessity.

The pious old fisherman, however, passed through it many a time undisturbed, when he was taking the choice fish, which he had caught at his beautiful home, to a large town situated not far from the confines of the forest. The principal reason why it was so easy for him to pass through this forest was because the tone of his thoughts was almost entirely of a religious character, and besides this, whenever he set foot upon the evil reputed shades, he was wont to sing some holy song, with a clear voice and a sincere heart.

While sitting over his nets this evening, unsuspicious of any evil, a sudden fear came upon him, at the sound of a rustling in the gloom of the forest, as of a horse and rider, the noise approaching nearer and nearer to the little promontory. All that he had dreamed, in many a stormy night, of the mysteries of the forest, now flashed at once through his mind ; foremost of all, the image of a gigantic snow-white man, who kept unceasingly nodding his head in a portentous manner. Indeed, when he raised his eyes towards the wood, it seemed to him as if he actually saw the nodding man approaching through the dense foliage. He soon however reassured himself, reflecting that nothing serious had ever befallen him even in the forest itself, and that upon this open tongue of land the evil spirit would be still less daring in the exercise of his power. At the same time he repeated aloud a text from the Bible with all his heart, and this so inspired him with courage that he almost smiled at the illusion he had allowed to possess him. The white nodding man was suddenly transformed into a brook long familiar to him, which ran foaming from the forest, and discharged itself into the lake. The noise however which he had heard, was caused by a knight beautifully apparelled, who, emerging from the deep shadows of the wood, came riding towards the cottage. A scarlet mantle was thrown over his purple gold-embroidered doublet ; a red and violet plume waved from his golden-coloured head-gear ; and a beautiful and richly ornamented sword flashed from his shoulder-belt. The white steed that bore the knight was more slenderly formed than war-horses generally are, and he stepped so lightly over the turf, that this green and flowery carpet seemed scarcely to receive the slightest injury from his tread.

The old fisherman did not however feel perfectly secure in his mind, although he tried to convince himself that no evil was to be feared from so graceful an apparition ; and therefore he politely took off his hat as the knight approached, and remained quietly with his nets.

7

Presently the stranger drew up, and enquired whether he and his horse could have shelter and care for the night. "As regards your horse, good sir," replied the fisherman, "I can assign him no better stable than this shady pasture, and no better provender than the grass growing on it. Yourself, however, I will gladly welcome to my small cottage, and give you supper and lodging as good as we have." The knight was well satisfied with this; he alighted from his horse, and, with the assistance of the fisherman, he relieved it from saddle and bridle, and turned it loose upon the flowery green. Then addressing his host he said : "Even had I found you less hospitable and kindly disposed, my worthy old fisherman, you would nevertheless scarcely have got rid of me to-day, for, as I see, a broad lake lies before us, and to ride back into that mysterious wood, with the shades of evening coming on, heaven keep me from it !" "We will not talk too much of that," said the fisherman, and he led his guest into the cottage.

There, beside the hearth, from which a scanty fire shed a dim light through the cleanly kept room, sat the fisherman's aged wife in a capacious chair. At the entrance of the noble guest she rose to give him a kindly welcome, but resumed her seat of honour without offering it to the stranger. Upon this the fisherman said with a smile : "You must not take it amiss of her, young sir, that she has not given up to you the most comfortable seat in the house ; it is a custom amongst poor people, that it should belong exclusively to the aged." "Why, husband," said the wife, with a quiet smile, "what can you be think-ing of? Our guest belongs no doubt to Christian men, and how could it come into the head of the good young blood to drive old people from their chairs? Take a seat, my young master," she con-tinued, turning towards the knight; "over there, there is a right pretty little chair, only you must not move about on it too roughly, for one of its legs is no longer of the firmest." The knight fetched the chair carefully, sat down upon it good-humouredly, and it seemed to him as if he were related to this little household, and had just returned from abroad.

The three worthy people now began to talk to-gether in the most friendly and familiar manner. With regard to the forest, about which the knight made some enquiries, the old man was not inclined to be communicative; he felt it was not a subject suited to approaching night, but the aged couple spoke freely of their home and former life, and lis-tened also gladly when the knight recounted to them his travels, and told them that he had a castle near the source of the Danube, and that his name was Sir Huldbrand of Ringstetten. During the conversation, the stranger had already occasionally heard a splash against the little low window, as if some one were sprinkling water against it. Every time the noise occurred, the old man knit his brow with displeasure; but when at last a whole shower was dashed against the panes, and bubbled into the room through the decayed casement, he rose angrily, and called threat-eningly from the window: "Undine! will you for once leave off these childish tricks? and to-day, be-

9

sides, there is a stranger knight with us in the cottage." All was silent without, only a suppressed laugh was audible, and the fisherman said as he returned : " You must pardon it in her, my honoured guest, and perhaps many a naughty trick besides ; but she means no harm by it. It is our foster-child Undine, and she will not wean herself from this childishness although she has already entered her eighteenth year. But, as I said, at heart she is thoroughly good."

" You may well talk," replied the old woman, shaking her head ; " when you come home from fishing or from a journey, her frolics may then be very delightful, but to have her about one the whole day long, and never to hear a sensible word, and instead of finding her a help in the housekeeping as she grows older, always to be obliged to be taking care that her follies do not completely ruin us, that is quite another thing, and the patience of a saint would be worn out at last." " Well, well," said her husband with a smile, " you have your troubles with Undine and I have mine with the lake. It often breaks away my dams, and tears my nets to pieces, but for all that, I have an affection for it, and so have you for the pretty child, in spite of all your crosses and vexations. Isn't it so ? " " One can't be very angry with her, certainly," said the old woman, and she smiled approvingly.

Just then the door flew open, and a beautiful fair girl glided laughingly into the room, and said : " You have only been jesting, father, for where is your guest ? "

At the same moment, however, she perceived the

AND·SWIFT·AS·AN ARROW·SHE·FLEW·

AND·FLED·INTO·THE·DARK·NIGHT·

knight, and stood fixed with astonishment before the handsome youth. Huldbrand was struck with her charming appearance, and dwelt the more earnestly on her lovely features, as he imagined it was only her surprise that gave him this brief enjoyment, and that she would presently turn from his gaze with increased bashfulness. It was, however, quite otherwise ; for after having looked at him for some time, she drew near him confidingly, knelt down before him, and said as she played with a gold medal which he wore on his breast, suspended from a rich chain : " Why, you handsome kind guest, how have you come to our poor cottage at last ? Have you been obliged then to wander through the world for years, before you could find your way to us ? Do you come out of that wild forest, my beautiful knight ? " The old woman's reproof allowed him no time for reply. She admonished the girl to stand up and behave herself and to go to her work. Undine, however, without making any answer drew a little foot-stool close to Huldbrand's chair, sat down upon it with her spinning, and said pleasantly : " I will work here." The old man did as parents are wont to do with spoilt children. He affected to observe nothing of Undine's naughtiness and was beginning to talk of something else. But this the girl would not let him do ; she said : " I have asked our charming guest whence he comes, and he has not yet answered me." " I come from the forest, you beautiful little vision," returned Huldbrand ; and she went on to say, " then you must tell me how you came there, for it is usually so feared, and what marvellous adventures you met with in it, for it is impossible to escape without something of the sort."

Huldbrand felt a slight shudder at this remembrance, and looked involuntarily towards the window, for it seemed to him as if one of the strange figures he had encountered in the forest were grinning in there ; but he saw nothing but the deep, dark night, which had now shrouded everything without. Upon this he composed himself and was on the point of beginning his little history, when the old man interrupted him by saying : " Not so, sir Knight ! this is no fit hour for such things." Undine, however, sprang angrily from her little stool, and standing straight before the fisherman with her fair arms fixed in her sides, she exclaimed : " He shall not tell his story, father ? He shall not ? but it is my will ! He shall ! He shall in spite of you ! " and thus saying she stamped her pretty little foot vehemently on the floor, but she did it all with such a comically graceful air, that Huldbrand now felt his gaze almost more riveted upon her in her anger, than before in her gentleness. The restrained wrath of the old man, on the contrary, burst forth violently. He severely reproved Undine's disobedience and unbecoming behaviour to the stranger, and his good old wife joined with him heartily. Undine quickly retorted, " If you want to chide me, and won't do what I wish, then sleep alone in your old smoky hut ! " and swift as an arrow she flew from the room, and fled into the dark night.

IN WHAT WAY UNDINE CAME TO THE FISHERMAN

CHAPTER II

IN WHAT WAY UNDINE HAD COME TO THE FISHERMAN

ULDBRAND and the fisherman sprang from their seats and were on the point of following the angry girl. Before they reached the cottage door, however, Undine had long vanished in the shadowy darkness without, and not even the sound of her light footstep betrayed the direction of her flight. Huldbrand looked enquiringly at his host ; it almost seemed to him as if the whole sweet apparition which had suddenly merged again into the night, were nothing else than one of that band of the wonderful forms which had, but a short time since, carried on their pranks with him in the forest. But

the old man murmured between his teeth : " This is not the first time that she has treated us in this way. Now we have aching hearts and sleepless eyes the whole night through ; for who knows that she may not some day come to harm, if she is thus out alone in the dark until daylight." " Then let us for God's sake follow her," cried Huldbrand anxiously. " What would be the good of it ? " replied the old man. " It would be a sin were I to allow you, all alone, to follow the foolish girl in the solitary night, and my old limbs would not overtake the wild runaway, even if we knew in what direction she had gone." " We had better at any rate call after her, and beg her to come back," said Huldbrand ; and he began to call in the most earnest manner : " Undine ! Undine ! Pray come back ! " The old man shook his head, saying, that all that shouting would help but little, for the knight had no idea how self-willed the little truant was. But still he could not forbear often calling out with him in the dark night : " Undine ! Ah ! dear Undine, I beg you to come back —only this once ! "

It turned out, however, as the fisherman had said. No Undine was to be heard or seen, and as the old man would on no account consent that Huldbrand should go in search of the fugitive, they were at last both obliged to return to the cottage. Here they found the fire on the hearth almost gone out, and the old wife, who took Undine's flight and danger far less to heart than her husband, had already retired to rest. The old man blew up the fire, laid some dry wood on it, and by the light of the flame sought out a tankard of wine, which he placed between himself and his guest. "You, Sir Knight," said he, "are also anxious about that silly girl, and we would both rather chatter and drink away a part of the night than keep turning round on our rush mats trying in vain to sleep. Is it not so?" Huldbrand was well satisfied with the plan, the fisherman obliged him to take the seat of honour vacated by the good old housewife, and both drank and talked together in a manner becoming two honest and trusting men. It is true, as often as the slightest thing moved before the windows, or even at times when nothing was moving, one of the two would look up and say: "She is coming!" Then they would be silent for a moment or two, and as nothing appeared, they would shake their heads and sigh and go on with their talk.

As, however, neither could think of anything but of Undine, they knew of nothing better to do, than that the old fisherman should tell the story, and the knight should hear, in what manner Undine had first come to the cottage. He therefore began as follows:

"It is now about fifteen years ago that I was one day crossing the wild forest with my goods, on my way to the city. My wife had stayed at home, as her wont is, and at this particular time for a very good reason, for God had given us in our tolerably advanced age, a wonderfully beautiful child. It was a little girl; and a question already arose between us, whether for the sake of the new comer, we would not leave our lovely home that we might better bring up this dear gift of heaven in some more habitable

place. Poor people indeed cannot do in such cases
as you may think they ought, Sir Knight, but, with
God's blessing, every one must do what he can.—
Well, the matter was tolerably in my head as I went
along. This slip of land was so dear to me, and I
shuddered when amidst the noise and brawls of the
city, I thought to myself, ' In such scenes as these, or
in one not much more quiet, thou wilt also soon
make thy abode ! ' But at the same time I did not
murmur against the good God, on the contrary, I
thanked Him in secret for the new-born babe ; I
should be telling a lie, too, were I to say, that on my
journey through the wood, going or returning, any
thing befell me out of the common way, and at that
time I had never seen any of its fearful wonders.
The Lord was ever with me in those mysterious
shades."

As he spoke he took his little cap from his bald
head, and remained for a time occupied with prayerful
thoughts ; he then covered himself again, and continued :

" On this side the forest, alas ! a sorrow awaited
me. My wife came to meet me with tearful eyes
and clad in mourning. ' Oh ! Good God ! ' I
groaned, ' where is our dear child ? speak ! ' ' With
Him on whom you have called, dear husband,' she
replied ; and we now entered the cottage together
weeping silently. I looked around for the little
corpse, and it was then only that I learned how it
had all happened.

" My wife had been sitting with the child on the
edge of the lake, and as she was playing with it, free

FOR GOD HAD GIVEN TO US
A WONDERFULLY BEAUTIFUL
CHILD.

of all fear and full of happiness, the little one suddenly bent forward, as if attracted by something very beautiful in the water. My wife saw her laugh, the dear angel, and stretch out her little hands ; but in a moment she had sprung out of her mother's arms, and had sunk beneath the watery mirror. I sought long for our little lost one ; but it was all in vain ; there was no trace of her to be found.

"The same evening we, childless parents, were sitting silently together in the cottage ; neither of us had any desire to talk, even had our tears allowed us. We sat gazing into the fire on the hearth. Presently, we heard something rustling outside the door ; it flew open, and a beautiful little girl three or four years old, richly dressed, stood on the threshold smiling at us. We were quite dumb with astonishment, and I knew not at first whether it were a vision or a reality. But I saw the water dripping from her golden hair and rich garments, and I perceived that the pretty child had been lying in the water, and needed help. 'Wife,' said I, 'no one has been able to save our dear child ; yet let us at any rate do for others, what would have made us so blessed.' We undressed the little one, put her to bed, and gave her something warm : at all this she spoke not a word and only fixed her eyes, that reflected the blue of the lake and of the sky, smilingly upon us.

"Next morning we quickly perceived that she had taken no harm from her wetting, and I now enquired about her parents, and how she had come here.

"But she gave a confused and strange account She must have been born far from here, not only because for these fifteen years I have not been able to find out anything of her parentage, but because she then spoke, and at times still speaks, of such singular things, that such as we are, cannot tell but that she may have dropped upon us from the moon. She talks of golden castles, of crystal domes, and heaven knows what besides. The story that she told with most distinctness was, that she was out in a boat with her mother on the great lake, and fell into the water, and that she only recovered her senses here under the trees where she felt herself quite happy on the merry shore.

"We had still a great misgiving and perplexity weighing on our hearts. We had indeed soon decided to keep the child we had found and to bring her up in the place of our lost darling ; but who could tell us whether she had been baptised or not ? She herself could give us no information on the matter. She generally answered our questions by saying that she well knew she was created for God's praise and glory, and that she was ready to let us do with her whatever would tend to His honour and glory.

"My wife and I thought that if she were not baptised, there was no time for delay, and that if she were, a good thing could not be repeated too often. And in pursuance of this idea, we reflected upon a good name for the child, for we now were often at a loss to know what to call her. We agreed at last that Dorothea would be most suitable for her, for I had once heard that it meant, *a gift of God*, and

FREE·OF·ALL·FEAR·AND·FULL·O
F·HAPPINESS·

she had surely been sent to us by God as a gift and comfort in our misery. She, on the other hand, would not hear of this, and told us that she thought she had been called Undine by her parents, and that Undine she wished still to be called. Now this appeared to me a heathenish name, not to be found in any calendar, and I took counsel therefore of a priest in the city. He also would not hear of the name of Undine, but at my earnest request he came with me through the mysterious forest in order to perform the rite of baptism here in my cottage. The little one stood before us so prettily arrayed and looked so charming, that the priest's heart was at once moved within him, and she flattered him so prettily, and braved hin so merrily that at last he could no longer remember the objections he had had ready against the name of Undine. She was therefore baptised 'Undine,' and during the sacred ceremony she behaved with great propriety and sweetness, wild and restless as she invariably was at other times. For my wife was quite right when she said that it has been hard to put up with her. If I were to tell you—"

The knight interrupted the fisherman to draw his attention to a noise, as of a rushing flood of waters, which had caught his ear during the old man's talk, and which now burst against the cottage-window with redoubled fury. Both sprang to the door. There they saw, by the light of the now risen moon, the brook which issued from the wood, wildly overflowing its banks, and whirling away stones and branches of trees in its sweeping course. The storm, as if

27

awakened by the tumult, burst forth from the mighty clouds which passed rapidly across the moon ; the lake roared under the furious lashing of the wind ; the trees of the little peninsula groaned from root to topmost bough, and bent, as if reeling, over the surging waters. "Undine ! for Heaven's sake, Undine !" cried the two men in alarm. No answer was returned, and regardless of every other consideration, they ran out of the cottage, one in this direction, and the other in that, searching and calling.

HOW THEY FOUND UNDINE AGAIN

"VENTURE NOT, VENTURE NOT, THE OLD MAN, THE STREAM, IS FULL OF TRICKS!"

CHAPTER III

HE longer Huldbrand sought Undine beneath the shades of night, and failed to find her, the more anxious and confused did he become. The idea, that Undine had been only a mere apparition of the forest again gained ascendency, over him ; indeed, amid the howling of the waves and the tempest, the cracking of the trees, and the complete transformation of a scene lately so calmly beautiful, he could almost have considered the whole peninsula with its cottage and its inhabitants as a mocking illusive vision ; but from afar he still ever heard through the tumult the fisherman's anxious call for Undine, and the loud praying and singing of his aged wife. At length he

31

came close to the brink of the swollen stream, and saw in the moonlight, how it had taken its wild course directly in front of the haunted forest, so as to change the peninsula into an island. "Oh God!" he thought to himself, "if Undine has ventured a step into that fearful forest, perhaps in her charming wilfulness, just because I was not allowed to tell her about it,—and now the stream may be rolling between us, and she may be weeping on the other side alone, among phantoms and spectres!" A cry of horror escaped him, and he clambered down some rocks and overthrown pine stems, in order to reach the rushing stream and by wading or swimming to seek the fugitive on the other side. He remembered all the awful and wonderful things which he had encountered even by day, under the now rustling and roaring branches of the forest. Above all it seemed to him, as if a tall man in white, whom he knew but too well, were grinning and nodding on the opposite shore ; but it was just these monstrous forms which forcibly impelled him to cross the flood, as the thought seized him that Undine might be among them in the agonies of death and alone.

He had already grasped the strong branch of a pine, and was standing supported by it, in the whirling current, against which he could with difficulty maintain himself ; though with a courageous spirit he advanced deeper into it. Just then a gentle voice exclaimed near him : "Venture not, venture not, the old man, the stream, is full of tricks!" He knew the sweet tones ; he stood as if entranced beneath the shadows that duskily shrouded the moon, and his head swam with the swelling of the waves, which he now saw rapidly rising to his waist. Still he would not desist.

"If thou art not really there, if thou art only floating about me like a mist, then may I too cease to live and become a shadow like thee, dear, dear Undine!" Thus exclaiming aloud, he again stepped deeper into the stream. "Look round thee, oh! look round thee, beautiful but infatuated youth!" cried a voice again close beside him, and looking aside, he saw by the momentarily unveiled moon, a little island formed by the flood, on which he perceived under the interweaved branches of the overhanging trees, Undine smiling and happy, nestling in the flowery grass.

Oh! how much more gladly than before did the young man now use the aid of his pine-branch!

With a few steps he had crossed the flood which was rushing between him and the maiden, and he was standing beside her on a little spot of turf, safely guarded and screened by the good old trees. Undine had half raised herself, and now under the green leafy tent she threw her arms round his neck, and drew him down beside her on her soft seat.

"You shall tell me your story here, beautiful friend," said she, in a low whisper; "the cross old people cannot hear us here; and our roof of leaves is just as good a shelter as their poor cottage." "It is heaven itself!" said Huldbrand, embracing the beautiful girl and kissing her fervently.

The old fisherman meanwhile had come to the

33   D

edge of the stream, and shouted across to the two young people : "Why, Sir Knight, I have received you as one honest-hearted man is wont to receive another, and now here you are caressing my foster-child in secret, and letting me run hither and thither through the night in anxious search of her." "I have only just found her myself, old father," returned the knight.

"So much the better," said the fisherman ; "but now bring her across to me without delay upon firm ground."

Undine however would not hear of this ; she declared she would rather go with the beautiful stranger into the wild forest itself, than return to the cottage, where no one did as she wished and from which the beautiful knight would himself depart sooner or later. Then, throwing her arms round Huldbrand, she sang with indescribable grace :

> "A Stream ran out of the misty vale
> Its fortunes to obtain,
> In the Ocean's depths it found a home
> And ne'er returned again."

The old fisherman wept bitterly at her song, but this did not seem to affect her particularly. She kissed and caressed her new friend, who at last said to her : "Undine, if the old man's distress does not touch your heart, it touches mine, let us go back to him." She opened her large blue eyes in amazement at him, and spoke at last slowly and hesitatingly : "If you think so,—well ; whatever you think is right to me. But the old man yonder must first

34

promise me that he will let you, without objection, relate to me what you saw in the wood, and—well, other things will settle themselves." " Come, only come," cried the fisherman to her, unable to utter another word ; at the same time he stretched out his arms far over the rushing stream towards her, and nodded his head as if to promise the fulfilment of her request, and as he did this, his white hair fell strangely over his face, and reminded Huldbrand of the nodding white man in the forest. Without allowing himself however to grow confused by such an idea the young knight took the beautiful girl in his arms, and bore her over the narrow passage which the stream had forced between her little island and the shore.

The old man fell upon Undine's neck and could not satisfy the exuberance of his joy ; his good wife also came up and caressed the newly-found in the heartiest manner. Not a word of reproach passed their lips ; nor was it thought of, for Undine, forgetting all her waywardness, almost overwhelmed her foster-parents with affection and fond expressions.

When at last they had recovered from the excess of their joy, day had already dawned, and had shed its purple hue over the lake ; stillness had followed the storm, and the little birds were singing merrily on the wet branches. As Undine now insisted upon hearing the knight's promised story, the aged couple smilingly and readily acceded to her desire. Breakfast was brought out under the trees which screened the cottage from the lake, and they sat down to it with contented hearts,—Undine on the grass at the knight's feet, the place chosen by herself.

Huldbrand then proceeded with his story.

FOURTH CHAPTER

Of that which the Knight encountered in the Wood.

CHAPTER IV

OF THAT WHICH THE KNIGHT ENCOUNTERED IN THE WOOD

"It is now about eight days ago since I rode into the free imperial city, which lies on the other side of the forest. Soon after my arrival, there was a splendid tournament and running at the ring, and I spared neither my horse nor my lance. Once when I was pausing at the lists, to rest after my merry toil, and was handing back my helmet to one of my squires, my attention was attracted by a female figure of great beauty, who was standing richly attired on one of the galleries allotted to spectators.

"I asked my neighbour, and learned from him, that the name of the fair lady was Bertalda, and that she was the foster-daughter of one of the powerful dukes living in the country. I remarked that she also was looking at me, and, as it is wont to be with us young knights, I had already ridden bravely, and now pursued my course with renovated confidence and courage. In the dance that evening I was Bertalda's partner, and I remained so throughout the festival."

A sharp pain in his left hand, which hung down

by his side, here interrupted Huldbrand's narrative, and drew his attention to the aching part. Undine had fastened her pearly teeth upon one of his fingers, appearing at the same time very gloomy and angry. Suddenly, however, she looked up in his eyes with an expression of tender melancholy, and whispered in a soft voice : "It is your own fault." Then she hid her face, and the knight, strangely confused and thoughtful, continued his narrative.

"This Bertalda was a haughty wayward girl. Even on the second day she pleased me no longer as she had done on the first, and on the third day still less. Still I continued about her, because she was more pleasant to me than to any other knight, and thus it was that I begged her in jest to give me one of her gloves. 'I will give it you when you have quite alone explored the ill-famed forest,' said she, 'and can bring me tidings of its wonders.' It was not that her glove was of such importance to me, but the word had been said, and an honourable knight would not allow himself to be urged a second time to such a proof of valour."

"I think she loved you," said Undine interrupting him.

"It seemed so," replied Huldbrand.

"Well," exclaimed the girl, laughing, "she must be stupid indeed. To drive away any one dear to her. And, moreover, into an ill-omened wood. The forest and its mysteries might have waited long enough for me!"

"Yesterday morning," continued the knight, smiling kindly at Undine, "I set out on my enter-

BERTA...A

prise. The stems of the trees caught the red tints of the morning light which lay brightly on the green turf, the leaves seemed whispering merrily with each other, and in my heart I could have laughed at the people who could have expected anything to terrify them in this pleasant spot. 'I shall soon have trotted through the forest there and back again,' I said to myself with a feeling of easy gaiety, and before I had even thought of it, I was deep within the green shades, and could no longer perceive the plain which lay behind me. Then for the first time it struck me that I might easily lose my way in the mighty forest, and that this perhaps was the only danger which the wanderer had to fear. I therefore paused and looked round in the direction of the sun, which in the meanwhile had risen somewhat higher above the horizon. While I was thus looking up, I saw something black in the branches of a lofty oak. I thought it was a bear, and I grasped my sword; but with a human voice, that sounded harsh and ugly, it called to me from above: 'If I do not nibble away the branches up here, Sir Malapert, what shall we have to roast you with at midnight?' And so saying it grinned, and made the branches rustle, so that my horse grew furious and rushed forward with me, before I had time to see what sort of a devil it really was."

"You must not call it so," said the old fisherman, as he crossed himself; his wife did the same silently; Undine looked at the knight with sparkling eyes and said: "The best of the story is, that they certainly have not roasted him yet; go on now, you beautiful youth!"

The knight continued his narration : " My horse was so wild, that he almost rushed with me against the stems and branches of trees ; he was dripping with sweat, and yet would not suffer himself to be held in. At last he went straight in the direction of a rocky precipice ; then it suddenly seemed to me, as if a tall white man threw himself across the path of my wild steed ; the horse trembled with fear and stopped ; I recovered my hold of him, and for the first time perceived that my deliverer was no white man but a brook of silvery brightness, rushing down from a hill by my side and crossing and impeding my horse's course."

" Thanks, dear Brook," exclaimed Undine, clapping her little hands. The old man, however, shook his head and looked down in deep thought.

" I had scarcely settled myself in the saddle," continued Huldbrand, " and seized the reins firmly, when a wonderful little man stood at my side, diminutive, and ugly beyond conception. His complexion was of a yellowish brown, and his nose not much smaller than the rest of his entire person. At the same time he kept grinning with stupid courtesy, exhibiting his huge mouth, and making a thousand scrapes and bows to me. As this farce was now becoming inconvenient to me, I thanked him briefly, and turned about my still trembling steed, thinking either to seek another adventure, or in case I met with none, to find my way back, for during my wild chase, the sun had already passed the meridian ; but the little fellow sprang round with the speed of lightning, and stood again before my horse. ' Room ! ' I cried angrily ; 'the animal is wild, and may easily run over you.' 'Ay, ay !' snarled the imp with a grin still more horribly stupid ; 'Give me first some drink-money, for I have stopped your horse ; without me, you and your horse would be now both lying in the stony ravine ; ugh !' 'Don't make any more faces,' said I, 'and take your money, even if you are telling lies ; for see, it was the good brook there that saved me, and not you, you miserable wight !' And at the same time I dropped a piece of gold into his grotesque cap, which he had taken off in his begging. I then trotted on ; but he screamed after me, and suddenly with inconceivable quickness was at my side. I urged my horse into a gallop ; the imp ran too, making at the same time strange contortions with his body, half ridiculous, half horrible, and holding up the gold-piece, he cried, at every leap, ' False money ! false coin ! false coin ! false money !'—and this he uttered with such a hollow sound, that one would have supposed that after every scream he would have fallen dead to the ground.

" His horrid red tongue moreover hung far out of his mouth. I stopped, perplexed, and asked : ' What do you mean by this screaming ? take another piece of gold, take two, but leave me.' He then began again his hideous burlesque of politeness, and snarled out : " Not gold, not gold, my young gentle-man, I have too much of that trash myself, as I will show you at once !'

"Suddenly it seemed to me as if I could see through the solid soil, as though it were green glass, and the smooth earth were as round as a ball ; and within, a multitude of goblins were making sport with silver and gold ; head over heels they were rolling about, pelting each other in jest with the precious metals, and provokingly blowing the gold-dust in each other's eyes. My hideous companion stood partly within and partly without ; he ordered the others to reach him up heaps of gold, and showing it to me with a laugh, he then flung it back again with a ringing noise into the immeasurable abyss.

"He then showed the piece of gold I had given him to the goblins below, and they laughed themselves half dead over it and hissed at me. At last they all pointed at me with their metal-stained fingers, and more and more wildly, and more and more densely, and more and more madly, the swarm of spirits came clambering up to me ;—I was seized with terror as my horse had been before ; I put spurs to him and I know not how far I galloped for the second time wildly into the forest.

"At length, when I again halted, the coolness of evening was around me. Through the branches of the trees I saw a white footpath gleaming, which I fancied must lead from the forest towards the city. I was anxious to work my way in that direction ; but a face perfectly white and indistinct, with features ever changing, kept peering at me between the leaves; I tried to avoid it, but wherever I went, it appeared also. Enraged at this, I determined at last to ride at it, when it gushed forth volumes of foam upon me and my horse, obliging us half-blinded to make a rapid retreat. Thus it drove us step by step ever away from the footpath, leaving the way open to us

only in one direction. When we advanced in this direction, it kept indeed close behind us, but did not do us the slightest harm.

"Looking round at it occasionally, I perceived that the white face that had besprinkled us with foam belonged to a form equally white and of gigantic stature. Many a time I thought that it was a moving stream, but I could never convince myself on the subject. Wearied out, the horse and his rider yielded to the impelling power of the white man, who kept nodding his head, as if he would say, 'Quite right, quite right!' And thus at last we came out here to the end of the forest, where I saw the turf, and the lake, and your little cottage, and where the tall white man disappeared."

"It's well that he's gone," said the old fisherman; and now he began to talk of the best way by which his guest could return to his friends in the city. Upon this Undine began to laugh slyly to herself; Huldbrand observed it, and said: "I thought you were glad to see me here; why then do you now rejoice when my departure is talked of?"

"Because you cannot go away," replied Undine. "Just try it once, to cross that overflowed forest stream with a boat, with your horse, or alone, as you may fancy. Or rather don't try it, for you would be dashed to pieces by the stones and trunks of trees which are carried down by it with the speed of lightning. And as to the lake, I know it well; Father dare not venture out far enough with his boat." Huldbrand rose, smiling, in order to see whether things were as Undine had said; the old man ac-

49   E

companied him, and the girl danced merrily along by
their side. They found everything indeed as Undine
had described, and the knight was obliged to submit
to remain on the little of tongue of land, that had
become an island, till the flood should subside. As
the three were returning to the cottage after their
ramble, the knight whispered in the ear of the little
maiden : " Well, how is it, my pretty Undine—are
you angry at my remaining ? " " Ah ! " she replied
peevishly, " let me alone. If I had not bitten you,
who knows how much of Bertalda would have appeared
in your story ? "

CHAPTER. V.

HOW. THE
KNIGHT LIVED
ON
THE LITTLE PROMONTORY

CHAPTER V

HOW THE KNIGHT LIVED ON THE LITTLE PROMONTORY

FTER having been much driven to and fro in the world, you have, perhaps, my dear reader, reached at length some spot where all was well with thee ; where the love for home and its calm peace, innate to all, has again sprung up within thee ; where thou hast thought that this home was rich with all the flowers of childhood and of the purest, deepest love that rests upon the graves of those that are gone, and thou hast felt it must be good to dwell here and to build habitations. Even if thou hast erred in this, and hast had afterwards bitterly to atone for the error, that is nothing to the purpose now, and thou wouldst not indeed voluntarily sadden thyself with the unpleasant recollection. But recall that

inexpressibly sweet foreboding, that angelic sense of peace, and thou wilt know somewhat of the knight Huldbrand's feelings during his abode on the little promontory.

He often perceived with hearty satisfaction that the forest stream rolled along every day more wildly, making its bed ever broader and broader, and prolonging his sojourn on the island to an indefinite period. Part of the day he rambled about with an old crossbow, which he had found in a corner of the cottage and had repaired ; and watching for the water-fowl, he killed all that he could for the cottage kitchen. When he brought his booty home, Undine rarely neglected to upbraid him with having so cruelly deprived the happy birds of life ; indeed, she often wept bitterly at the sight he placed before her. But if he came home another time without having shot anything, she scolded him no less seriously, since now, from his carelessness and want of skill, they had to be satisfied with living on fish. He always delighted heartily in her graceful little scoldings, all the more as she generally strove to compensate for her ill humour by the sweetest caresses.

The old people took pleasure in the intimacy of the young pair ; they regarded them as betrothed, or even as already united in marriage, and living on this isolated spot, as a succour and support to them in their old age. It was this same sense of seclusion that suggested the idea also to Huldbrand's mind that he was already Undine's accepted one. He felt as if there were no world beyond the surrounding waters, or as if he could never recross them to mingle

with other men ; and when at times his grazing horse would neigh as if enquiringly to remind him of knightly deeds, or when the coat of arms on his embroidered saddle and horse-gear shone sternly upon him, or when his beautiful sword would suddenly fall from the nail on which it was hanging in the cottage, gliding from the scabbard as it fell,—he would quiet the doubts of his mind by saying :—" Undine is no fisherman's daughter ; she belongs in all probability to some illustrious family abroad." There was only one thing to which he had a strong aversion, and this was, when the old dame reproved Undine in his presence. The wayward girl, it is true, laughed at it for the most part, without attempting to conceal her mirth ; but it seemed to him as if his honour were concerned, and yet he could not blame the old fisher-man's wife, for Undine always deserved at least ten times as many reproofs as she received ; so in his heart he felt the balance in favour of the old woman, and his whole life flowed onwards in calm enjoy-ment.

There came, however, an interruption at last. The fisherman and the knight had been accustomed at their mid-day meal, and also in the evening when the wind roared without, as it was always wont to do towards night, to enjoy together a flask of wine. But now the store which the fisherman had from time to time brought with him from the town, was ex-hausted, and the two men were quite out of humour in consequence.

Undine laughed at them excessively all day, but they were neither of them merry enough to join in her jests as usual. Towards evening she went out of the cottage to avoid, as she said, two such long and tiresome faces. As twilight advanced, there were again tokens of a storm, and the water rushed and roared. Full of alarm, the knight and the fisherman sprang to the door, to bring home the girl, remembering the anxiety of that night when Huldbrand had first come to the cottage. Undine, however, met them, clapping her little hands with delight. "What will you give me," she said, "to provide you with wine?" or rather, "you need not give me anything," she continued, "for I am satisfied if you will look merrier and be in better spirits than you have been throughout this whole wearisome day. Only come with me; the forest stream has driven ashore a cask, and I will be condemned to sleep through a whole week if it is not a wine-cask." The men followed her, and in a sheltered creek on the shore, they actually found a cask, which inspired them with the hope that it contained the generous drink for which they were thirsting.

They at once rolled it as quickly as possible towards the cottage, for the western sky was overcast with heavy storm-clouds, and they could observe in the twilight the waves of the lake raising their white foaming heads, as if looking out for the rain which was presently to pour down upon them. Undine helped the men as much as she was able, and when the storm of rain suddenly burst over them, she said, with a merry threat to the heavy clouds : "Come, come, take care that you don't wet us ; we are still some way from shelter." The old man reproved her for this, as simple presumption, but she laughed softly to herself, and no mischief befell any one in consequence of her levity. Nay, more ; contrary to all expectation, they reached the comfortable hearth with their booty perfectly dry, and it was not till they had opened the cask, and had proved that it contained some wonderfully excellent wine, that the rain burst forth from the dark cloud, and the storm raged among the tops of the trees, and over the agitated billows of the lake.

Several bottles were soon filled from the great cask which promised a supply for many days, and they were sitting drinking and jesting round the glowing fire, feeling comfortably secured from the raging storm without. Suddenly the old fisherman became very grave and said : " Ah, great God ! here are we rejoicing over this rich treasure, and he to whom it once belonged and of whom the floods have robbed it, has probably lost his precious life in their waters." " That he has not," declared Undine, and she smilingly filled the knight's cup to the brim. But Huldbrand replied, " By my honour, old father, if I knew where to find and to rescue him, no knightly errand and no danger would I shirk. So much, however, I can promise you, that if ever again I reach more inhabited lands, I will find out the owner of this wine or his heirs, and requite it twofold, nay, threefold." This delighted the old man ; he nodded approvingly to the knight, and drained his cup with a better conscience and greater pleasure. Undine, however, said to Huldbrand : " Do as you will with your gold and your reimbursement ; but you spoke

foolishly about the venturing out in search ; I should cry my eyes out, if you were lost in the attempt, and isn't it true, that you would yourself rather stay with me and the good wine ? " " Yes, indeed," answered Huldbrand, smiling. "Then," said Undine, " you spoke unwisely. For charity begins at home, and what do other people concern us ? " The old woman turned away sighing and shaking her head ; the fisherman forgot his wonted affection for the pretty girl, and scolded her. " It sounds exactly," said he, as he finished his reproof, " as if Turks and heathens had brought you up ; may God forgive both me and you, you spoiled child." "Well," replied Undine, "for all that, it is what I feel, let who will have brought me up, and all your words can't help that." " Silence ! " exclaimed the fisherman, and Undine, who in spite of her pertness, was exceedingly fearful, shrank from him, and moving tremblingly towards Huldbrand, asked him in a soft tone : " Are you also angry, dear friend ? " The knight pressed her tender hand and stroked her hair. He could say nothing, for vexation at the old man's severity towards Undine closed his lips ; and thus the two couple sat opposite to each other, with angry feelings and embarrassed silence.

OF A NUPTIAL CEREMONY

CHAPTER VI

A LOW knocking at the door was heard in the midst of this stillness, startling all the inmates of the cottage ; for there are times when a little circumstance, happening quite unexpectedly, can unduly alarm us. But there was here the additional cause of alarm that the enchanted forest lay so near, and that the little promontory seemed just now inaccessible to human beings. They looked at each other doubtingly, as the knocking was repeated accompanied by a deep groan, and the knight sprang to reach his sword. But the old

65   F

man whispered softly : "If it be what I fear, no weapon will help us." Undine meanwhile approached the door and called out angrily and boldly : "Spirits of the earth, if you wish to carry on your mischief, Kühleborn shall teach you something better." The terror of the rest was increased by these mysterious words ; they looked fearfully at the girl, and Huldbrand was just regaining courage enough to ask what she meant, when a voice said without : "I am no spirit of the earth, but a spirit indeed still within its earthly body. You within in the cottage, if you fear God and will help me, open to me." At these words, Undine had already opened the door, and had held a lamp out in the stormy night, by which they perceived an aged priest standing there, who stepped back in terror at the unexpected sight of the beautiful maiden. He might well think that witchcraft and magic were at work when such a lovely form appeared at such an humble cottage door ; he therefore began to pray : "All good spirits praise the Lord ! " " I am no spectre," said Undine smiling ; · " do I then look so ugly ? Besides you may see the holy words do not frighten me. I too know of God, and understand how to praise Him ; every one to be sure in his own way, for so He has created us. Come in, venerable father ; you come among good people."

The holy man entered, bowing and looking round him, with a profound yet tender demeanour. But the water was dropping from every fold of his dark garment, and from his long white beard and from his grey locks. The fisherman and the knight took him to another apartment and furnished him with other clothes,

while they gave the women his own wet attire to dry.
The aged stranger thanked them humbly and cour-
teously, but he would on no account accept the knight's
splendid mantle, which was offered to him ; but he
chose instead an old grey over-coat belonging to the
fisherman. They then returned to the apartment, and
the good old dame immediately vacated her easy chair
for the reverend father, and would not rest till he had
taken possession of it ; " For," said she, " you are old
and exhausted, and you are moreover a man of God."
Undine pushed under the stranger's feet her little stool,
on which she had been wont to sit by the side of
Huldbrand, and she showed herself in every way most
gentle and kind in her care of the good old man.
Huldbrand whispered some raillery at it in her ear, but
she replied very seriously : " He is a servant of Him
who created us all ; holy things are not to be jested
with." The knight and the fisherman then refreshed
their reverend guest with food and wine, and when he
had somewhat recovered himself, he began to relate
how he had the day before set out from his cloister,
which lay far beyond the great lake, intending to
travel to the Bishop, in order to acquaint him with
the distress into which the monastery and its tributary
villages had fallen on account of the extraordinary
floods.

After a long circuitous route, which these very
floods had obliged him to take, he had been this day
compelled towards evening, to procure the aid of a
couple of good boatmen to cross an arm of the lake,
which had overflowed its banks. " Scarcely however,"
continued he, " had our small craft touched the waves,

than that furious tempest burst forth which is now raging over our heads.

"It seemed as if the waters had only waited for us, to commence their wildest whirling dance with our little boat. The oars were soon torn out of the hands of my men, and were dashed by the force of the waves further and further beyond our reach. We ourselves, yielding to the resistless powers of nature, helplessly drifted over the surging billows of the lake towards your distant shore, which we already saw looming through the mist and foam. Presently our boat turned round and round as in a giddy whirlpool; I know not whether it was upset, or whether I fell over-board. In a vague terror of inevitable death I drifted on, till a wave cast me here, under the trees on your island."

"Yes, island!" cried the fisherman; "a short time ago it was only a point of land; but now, since the forest-stream and the lake have become well-nigh bewitched, things are quite different with us."

"I remarked something of the sort," said the priest, "as I crept along the shore in the dark, and hearing nothing but the uproar around me, I at last perceived that a beaten footpath disappeared just in the direction from which the sound proceeded. I now saw the light in your cottage, and ventured hither, and I cannot sufficiently thank my heavenly Father that after preserving me from the waters, He has led me to such good and pious people as you are; and I feel this all the more, as I do not know whether I shall ever behold any other beings in this world, except those I now address."

68

"What do you mean?" asked the fisherman.

"Do you know then how long this commotion of the elements is to last?" replied the holy man. "And I am old in years. Easily enough may the stream of my life run itself out before the overflowing of the forest-stream may subside. And indeed it were not impossible that more and more of the foaming waters may force their way between you and yonder forest, until you are so far sundered from the rest of the world that your little fishing-boat will no longer be sufficient to carry you across, and the inhabitants of the continent in the midst of their diversions will have entirely forgotten you in your old age."

The fisherman's wife started at this, crossed herself and exclaimed, "God forbid!" But her husband looked at her with a smile, and said : "What creatures we are after all! even were it so, things would not be very different—at least not for you, dear wife—than they now are. For have you for many years been further than the edge of the forest? and have you seen any other human beings than Undine and myself? The knight and this holy man have only come to us lately. They will remain with us if we do become a forgotten island ; so you would even be a gainer by it after all."

"I don't know," said the old woman ; "it is somehow a gloomy thought, when one imagines that one is separated for ever from other people, although, were it otherwise, one might neither know nor see them."

"Then you will remain with us ! then you will

69

remain with us !'' whispered Undine in a low half singing tone, as she nestled closer to Huldbrand's side. But he was absorbed in the deep and strange visions of his own mind.

The region on the other side of the forest-river seemed to dissolve into distance during the priest's last words ; and the blooming island upon which he lived, grew more green, and smiled more freshly in his mind's vision. His beloved one glowed as the fairest rose of this little spot of earth, and even of the whole world, and the priest was actually there. Added to this, at that moment an angry glance from the old dame was directed at the beautiful girl, because even in the presence of the reverend father she leant so closely on the knight, and it seemed as if a torrent of reproving words were on the point of following. Presently, turning to the priest, Huldbrand broke forth : " Venerable father, you see before you here a pair pledged to each other ; and if this maiden and these good old people have no objection, you shall unite us this very evening." The aged couple were extremely surprised. They had, it is true, hitherto often thought of something of the sort, but they had never yet expressed it, and when the knight now spoke thus, it came upon them as something wholly new and unprecedented.

Undine had become suddenly grave, and looked down thoughtfully while the priest enquired respecting the circumstances of the case, and asked if the old people gave their consent. After much discussion together, the matter was settled ; the old dame went to arrange the bridal chamber for the young people, and to look out two consecrated tapers which she had had in her possession for some time, and which she thought essential to the nuptial ceremony. The knight in the meanwhile examined his gold chain, from which he wished to disengage two rings, that he might make an exchange of them with his bride.

She, however, observing what he was doing, started up from her reverie, and exclaimed : " Not so ! my parents have not sent me into the world quite destitute ; on the contrary, they must have anticipated with certainty that such an evening as this would come." Thus saying, she quickly left the room and reappeared in a moment with two costly rings, one of which she gave to her bridegroom, and kept the other for herself. The old fisherman was extremely astonished at this, and still more so his wife, who just then entered, for neither had ever seen these jewels in the child's possession.

" My parents," said Undine, " sewed these little things into the beautiful frock which I had on, when I came to you. They forbade me, moreover, to mention them to any one before my wedding evening, so I secretly took them, and kept them concealed until now." The priest interrupted all further questionings, by lighting the consecrated tapers, which he placed upon a table, and summoned the bridal pair to stand opposite to him. He then gave them to each other with a few short solemn words ; the elder couple gave their blessing to the younger, and the bride, trembling and thoughtful, leaned upon the knight. Then the priest suddenly said : " You are strange people after all ! Why did you tell me you were the only people here on the island ? and during the whole ceremony, a tall stately man in a white mantle has been looking at me through the window opposite. He must still be standing before the door, to see if you will invite him to come into the house." "God forbid !" said the old dame with a start ; the fisherman shook his head in silence, and Huldbrand sprang to the window. It seemed even to him as if he could still see a white streak, but it soon completely disappeared in the darkness. He convinced the priest that he must have been absolutely mistaken and they all sat down together round the hearth.

WHAT FURTHER HAPPENED ON THE EVENING OF THE WEDDING

CHAPTER VII

OTH before and during the ceremony Undine had shown herself gentle and quiet ; but it now seemed as if all the wayward humours which rioted within her, burst forth all the more boldly and unrestrainedly. She teased her bridegroom and her foster-parents, and even the holy man whom she had so lately reverenced, with all sorts of childish tricks ; and when the old woman was about to reprove her, she was quickly silenced by a few grave words from the knight, speaking of Undine now as his wife. Nevertheless the knight himself was equally little pleased with Undine's childish behaviour ; but no signs, and no reproachful words were of any avail.

It is true, whenever the bride noticed her husband's dissatisfaction—and this occurred occasionally—she became more quiet, sat down by his side, caressed him, whispered something smilingly into his ear, and smoothed the wrinkles that were gathering on his brow. But immediately afterwards, some wild freak would again lead her to return to her ridiculous proceedings, and matters would be worse than before. At length the priest said in a serious and kind tone : "My fair young maiden, no one indeed can look at you without delight ; but remember so to attune your soul betimes, that it may ever harmonise with that of your wedded husband." "Soul !" said Undine laughing ; "that sounds pretty enough, and may be a very edifying and useful caution for most people. But when one hasn't a soul at all, I beg you, what is there to attune then ? and that is my case." The priest was silent and deeply wounded, and with holy displeasure he turned his face from the girl. She however went up to him caressingly and said : "No ! listen to me first, before you look angry, for your look of anger gives me pain, and you must not give pain to any creature, who has done you no wrong—only have patience with me, and I will tell you properly what I mean."

It was evident that she was preparing herself to explain something in detail, but suddenly she hesitated, as if seized with an inward shuddering, and burst out into a flood of tears. They none of them knew what to make of this ebullition, and filled with various apprehensions they gazed at her in silence. At length, wiping away her tears, and looking

earnestly at the reverend man, she said : " There must be something beautiful, but at the same time extremely awful about a soul. Tell me, holy Sir, were it not better that we never shared such a gift ? " She was silent again, as if waiting for an answer, and her tears had ceased to flow. All in the cottage had risen from their seats and had stepped back from her with horror. She however seemed to have eyes for no one but the holy man ; her features wore an expression of fearful curiosity, which appeared terrible to those who saw her. " The soul must be a heavy burden," she continued, as no one answered her, " very heavy ! for even its approaching image overshadows me with anxiety and sadness. And, ah ! I was so light-hearted and so merry till now ! " And she burst into a fresh flood of tears, and covered her face with the drapery she wore. Then the priest went up to her with a solemn air, and spoke to her, and conjured her by the name of the Most Holy to cast aside the veil that enveloped her, if any spirit of evil possessed her. But she sank on her knees before him, repeating all the sacred words he uttered, praising God, and protesting that she wished well with the whole world. Then at last the priest said to the knight : " Sir bridegroom, I will leave you alone with her whom I have united to you in marriage. So far as I can discover there is nothing of evil in her, but much indeed that is mysterious. I commend to you—prudence, love, and fidelity." So saying, he went out, and the fisherman and his wife followed him crossing themselves.

Undine had sunk on her knees ; she unveiled her

79

face and said, looking timidly round on Huldbrand:
"Alas! you will surely now not keep me as your
own; and yet I have done no evil, poor child that I
am!" As she said this, she looked so exquisitely
graceful and touching, that her bridegroom forgot
all the horror he had felt, and all the mystery that
clung to her, and hastening to her he raised her in
his arms. She smiled through her tears; it was a
smile like the morning-light playing on a little
stream. "You cannot leave me," she whispered
with confident security, stroking the knight's cheek
with her tender hand. Huldbrand tried to dismiss
the fearful thoughts that still lurked in the back-
ground of his mind, persuading him that he was
married to a fairy or to some malicious and mis-
chievous being of the spirit world, only the single
question half unawares escaped his lips: "My little
Undine, tell me this one thing, what was it you said
of spirits of the earth and of Kühleborn, when the
priest knocked at the door?" "It was nothing but
fairy-tales!—children's fairy-tales!" said Undine,
with all her wonted gaiety; "I frightened you at
first with them, and then you frightened me, that's
the end of our story and of our nuptial evening."
"Nay! that it isn't," said the knight, intoxicated
with love, and extinguishing the tapers, he bore his
beautiful beloved to the bridal chamber by the light
of the moon which shone brightly through the
windows.

THE DAY AFTER THE WEDDING.

CHAPTER VIII

THE DAY AFTER THE WEDDING

HE fresh light of the morning awoke the young married pair. Wonderful and horrible dreams had disturbed Huldbrand's rest; he had been haunted by spectres, who, grinning at him by stealth, had tried to disguise themselves as beautiful women, and from beautiful women they all at once assumed the faces of dragons, and when he started up from these hideous visions, the moonlight shone pale and cold into the room; terrified he looked at Undine, who still lay in unaltered beauty and grace. Then he would press a light kiss upon her rosy lips, and would fall asleep again only to be awakened by new terrors. After he had reflected on all this, now that he was fully awake, he reproached himself for any doubt that could have

led him into error with regard to his beautiful wife. He begged her to forgive him for the injustice he had done her, but she only held out to him her fair hand, sighed deeply and remained silent. But a glance of exquisite fervour beamed from her eyes such as he had never seen before, carrying with it the full assurance that Undine bore him no ill-will. He then rose cheerfully and left her, to join his friends in the common apartment.

He found the three sitting round the hearth, with an air of anxiety about them, as if they dared not venture to speak aloud. The priest seemed to be praying in his inmost spirit that all evil might be averted. When, however, they saw the young husband come forth so cheerfully, the careworn expression of their faces vanished.

The old fisherman even began to jest with the knight, so pleasantly, that the aged wife smiled good-humouredly as she listened to them. Undine at length made her appearance. All rose to meet her, and all stood still with surprise, for the young wife seemed so strange to them and yet the same. The priest was the first to advance towards her, with paternal affection beaming in his face, and, as he raised his hand to bless her, the beautiful woman sank reverently on her knees before him. With a few humble and gracious words, she begged him to forgive her for any foolish things she might have said the evening before, and entreated him in an agitated tone to pray for the welfare of her soul. She then rose, kissed her foster-parents, and thanking them for all the goodness they had shown her, she exclaimed :

"Oh! I now feel in my innermost heart, how much, how infinitely much, you have done for me, dear, kind people!" She could not at first desist from her caresses, but scarcely had she perceived that the old woman was busy in preparing breakfast, than she went to the hearth, cooked and arranged the meal, and would not suffer the good old mother to take the least trouble.

She continued thus throughout the whole day, quiet, kind, and attentive,—at once a little matron and a tender, bashful girl. The three who had known her longest, expected every moment to see some whimsical vagary of her capricious spirit burst forth. But they waited in vain for it. Undine remained as mild and gentle as an angel. The holy father could not take his eyes from her, and he said repeatedly to the bridegroom : "The goodness of heaven, sir, has entrusted a treasure to you yesterday through me, unworthy as I am ; cherish it as you ought, and it will promote your temporal and eternal welfare."

Towards evening, Undine was hanging on the knight's arm with humble tenderness, and drew him gently out of the door, where the declining sun was shining pleasantly on the fresh grass, and upon the tall slender stems of the trees. The eyes of the young wife were moist, as with the dew of sadness and love, and a tender and fearful secret seemed hovering on her lips, which however was only disclosed by scarcely audible sighs. She led her husband onward and onward in silence ; when he spoke, she only answered him with looks, in which, it is true,

87

there lay no direct reply to his enquiries, but a whole
heaven of love and timid devotion. Thus they
reached the edge of the swollen forest-stream, and
the knight was astonished to see it rippling along
in gentle waves, without a trace of its former wild-
ness and swell. "By the morning it will be quite
dry," said the beautiful wife, in a regretful tone,
"and you can then travel away wherever you will,
without anything to hinder you." "Not without
you, my little Undine," replied the knight, laughing ;
"remember, even if I wished to desert you, the
church, and the spiritual powers, and the emperor,
and the empire, would interpose and bring the fugitive back again." "All depends upon you, all depends
upon you," whispered his wife, half weeping, and half
smiling. "I think, however, nevertheless, that you
will keep me with you ; I love you so heartily. Now
carry me across to that little island, that lies before
us. The matter shall be decided there. I could easily
indeed glide through the rippling waves, but it is so
restful in your arms, and if you were to cast me off, I
shall have sweetly rested in them once more for the
last time." Huldbrand, full as he was of strange fear
and emotion, knew not what to reply. He took her
in his arms and carried her across, remembering now
for the first time that this was the same little island
from which he had borne her back to the old fisherman on that first night. On the farther side, he put
her down on the soft grass and was on the point of
placing himself lovingly near his beautiful burden,
when she said : "No, there, opposite to me ! I will
read my sentence in your eyes, before your lips speak ;

88

now, listen attentively to what I will relate to you."
And she began :

" You must know, my loved one, that there are
beings in the elements which almost appear like mortals, and which rarely allow themselves to become
visible to your race. Wonderful salamanders glitter
and sport in the flames ; lean and malicious gnomes
dwell deep within the earth ; spirits, belonging to
the air, wander through the forests ; and a vast
family of water spirits live in the lakes and streams
and brooks. In resounding domes of crystal, through
which the sky looks in with its sun and stars, these
latter spirits find their beautiful abode ; lofty trees
of coral with blue and crimson fruits gleam in their
gardens ; they wander over the pure sand of the sea,
and among lovely variegated shells, and amid all
exquisite treasures of the old world, which the present
is no longer worthy to enjoy ; all these the floods
have covered with their secret veils of silver, and the
noble monuments sparkle below, stately and solemn,
and bedewed by the loving waters which allure from
them many a beautiful moss-flower and entwining
cluster of sea grass. Those, however, who dwell
there, are very fair and lovely to behold, and for the
most part, are more beautiful than human beings.
Many a fisherman has been so fortunate as to surprise
some tender mermaid, as she rose above the waters
and sang. He would then tell afar of her beauty,
and such wonderful beings have been given the name
of Undines. You, however, are now actually be-
holding an Undine."

The knight tried to persuade himself that his

beautiful wife was under the spell of one of her strange humours, and that she was taking pleasure in teasing him with one of her extravagant inventions. But repeatedly as he said this to himself, he could not believe it for a moment ; a strange shudder passed through him ; unable to utter a word, he stared at the beautiful narrator with an immovable gaze. Undine shook her head sorrowfully, drew a deep sigh, and then proceeded as follows :

"Our condition would be far superior to that of other human beings,—for human beings we call ourselves, being similar to them in form and culture,—but there is one evil peculiar to us. We and our like in the other elements, vanish into dust, and pass away, body and spirit, so that not a vestige of us remains behind ; and when you mortals hereafter awake to a purer life, we remain with the sand and the sparks and the wind and the waves. Hence we have also no souls ; the element moves us, and is often obedient to us while we live, though it scatters us to dust when we die ; and we are merry, without having aught to grieve us,—merry as the nightingales and little gold-fishes and other pretty children of nature. But all beings aspire to be higher than they are. Thus my father, who is a powerful water-prince in the Mediterranean Sea, desired that his only daughter should become possessed of a soul, even though she must then endure many of the sufferings of those thus endowed. Such as we are, however, can only obtain a soul by the closest union of affection with one of your human race. I am now possessed of a soul, and my soul thanks you, my inexpressibly

beloved one, and it will ever thank you, if you do not make my whole life miserable. For what is to become of me, if you avoid and reject me? Still I would not retain you by deceit. And if you mean to reject me, do so now, and return alone to the shore. I will dive into this brook, which is my uncle; and here in the forest, far removed from other friends, he passes his strange and solitary life. He is however powerful, and is esteemed and beloved by many great streams; and as he brought me hither to the fisherman, a light-hearted laughing child, he will take me back again to my parents, a loving, suffering, and soul-endowed woman."

She was about to say still more, but Huldbrand embraced her with the most heartfelt emotion and love, and bore her back again to the shore. It was not till he reached it, that he swore amid tears and kisses, never to forsake his sweet wife, calling himself more happy than the Greek Pygmalion, whose beautiful statue received life from Venus and became his loved one. In endearing confidence, Undine walked back to the cottage, leaning on his arm; feeling now for the first time with all her heart, how little she ought to regret the forsaken crystal palaces of her mysterious father.

HOW THE KNIGHT
TOOK HIS YOUNG
WIFE WITH HIM.

CHAPTER IX.

HOW THE KNIGHT TOOK HIS YOUNG WIFE WITH HIM.

HEN Huldbrand awoke from his sleep on the following morning, and missed h i s beautiful wife from his side, he began to indulge again in the strange thoughts, that his marriage and the charming Undine herself were but fleeting and deceptive illusions. But at the same moment she entered the room, sat down beside him, and said : "I have been out rather early, to see if my uncle keeps his word. He has already led all the waters back again into his own calm channel, and he now flows through the forest, solitarily and dreamily as before. His friends in the water and the air have also returned to repose ; all

will again go on quietly and regularly, and you can travel homeward when you will, dry-shod." It seemed to Huldbrand as though he were in a waking dream, so little could he reconcile himself to the strange relationship of his wife. Nevertheless he made no remark on the matter, and the exquisite grace of his bride soon lulled to rest every uneasy misgiving. When he was afterwards standing before the door with her, and looking over the green penin-sula with its boundary of clear waters, he felt so happy in this cradle of his love, that he exclaimed : " Why shall we travel so soon as to-day ? We shall scarcely find more pleasant days in the world yonder, than those we have spent in this quiet little shelter. Let us yet see the sun go down here, twice or thrice more." "As my lord wills," replied Undine humbly. " It is only that the old people will, at all events, part from me with pain, and when they now for the first time perceive the true soul within me, and how I can now heartily love and honour, their feeble eyes will be dimmed with plentiful tears. At present they consider my quietness and gentleness of no better promise than before, like the calmness of the lake when the air is still ; and as matters now are, they will soon learn to cherish a flower or a tree as they have cherished me. Do not therefore let me reveal to them this newly-bestowed and loving heart, just at the moment when they must lose it for this world ; and how could I conceal it, if we remain longer together ? "

Huldbrand conceded the point ; he went to the aged people and talked with them over the journey, which he proposed to undertake immediately. The holy father offered to accompany the young married pair, and after a hasty farewell, he and the knight assisted the beautiful bride to mount her horse, and walked with rapid step by her side over the dry channel of the forest stream into the wood beyond. Undine wept silently but bitterly, and the old people gave loud expression to their grief. It seemed as if they had a presentiment of all they were now losing in their foster-child.

The three travellers had reached in silence the densest shades of the forest. It must have been a fair sight under that green canopy of leaves, to see Undine's lovely form, as she sat on her noble and richly ornamented steed, with the venerable priest in the white garb of his order on one side of her, and on the other the blooming young knight in his gay and splendid attire with his sword at his girdle. Huldbrand had no eyes but for his beautiful wife ; Undine, who had dried her tears, had no eyes but for him, and they soon fell into a mute, voiceless converse of glance and gesture, from which they were only roused at length by the low talking of the reverend father with a fourth traveller, who in the meanwhile had joined them unobserved.

He wore a white garment almost resembling the dress of the priest's order, except that his hood hung low over his face, and his whole attire floated round him in such vast folds, that he was obliged every moment to gather it up, and throw it over his arm, or dispose of it in some way, and yet it did not in the least seem to impede his movements. When the young couple first perceived him, he was just saying : " And so, venerable sir, I have now dwelt for many years here in the forest, and yet no one

could call me a hermit, in your sense of the word. For as I said, I know nothing of penance, and I do not think I have any especial need of it. I love the forest only for this reason, that its beauty is quite peculiar to itself, and it amuses me to pass along in my flowing white garments among the leaves and dusky shadows, while now and then a sweet sunbeam shines down unexpectedly upon me." "You are a very strange man," replied the priest, "and I should like to be more closely acquainted with you." "And to pass from one thing to another, who may you be yourself?" asked the stranger. "I am called Father Heilmann," said the holy man; "and I come from the monastery of 'our Lady' which lies on the other side of the lake." "Indeed," replied the stranger; "my name is Kühleborn, and so far as courtesy is concerned, I might claim the title of Lord of Kühleborn, or free Lord of Kühleborn; for I am as free as the birds of the forest and perhaps a little more so. For example, I have now something to say to the young lady there." And before they were aware of his intention, he was at the other side of the priest, close beside Undine, stretching himself up to whisper something in her ear. But she turned from him with alarm, and exclaimed: "I have nothing more to do with you." "Ho, ho," laughed the stranger, "what is this immensely grand marriage you have made, that you don't know your own relations any longer? Have you forgotten your uncle Kühleborn, who so faithfully bore you on his back through this region?" "I beg you, nevertheless," replied Undine, "not to appear in my presence again. I am now afraid of you; and suppose my husband should learn to avoid me when he sees me in such strange company and with such relations!" "My little niece," said Kühleborn, "you must not forget that I

am with you here as a guide ; the spirits of earth
that haunt this place might otherwise play some of
their stupid pranks with you. Let me therefore go
quietly on with you ; the old priest there remembered me better than you appear to have done, for he
assured me just now that I seemed familiar to him,
and that I must have been with him in the boat, out
of which he fell into the water. I was so, truly
enough ; for I was the water-spout that carried him
out of it and washed him safely ashore for your
wedding."

Undine and the knight turned towards Father
Heilmann ; but he seemed walking on, as in a sort
of dream, and no longer to be conscious of all that
was passing. Undine then said to Kühleborn : " I
see yonder the end of the forest. We no longer need
your help, and nothing causes us alarm but yourself.
I beg you, therefore, in all love and good will, vanish,
and let us proceed in peace. Kühleborn seemed to
become angry at this ; his countenance assumed a
frightful expression, and he grinned fiercely at
Undine, who screamed aloud and called upon her
husband for assistance. As quick as lightning, the
knight sprang to the other side of the horse, and
aimed his sharp sword at Kühleborn's head. But the
sword cut through a water-fall, which was rushing
down near them from a lofty crag ; and with a
splash, which almost sounded like a burst of laughter,
it poured over them and wet them through to the skin.
The priest, as if suddenly awaking, exclaimed : " I
have long been expecting that, for the stream ran
down from the height so close to us. At first it

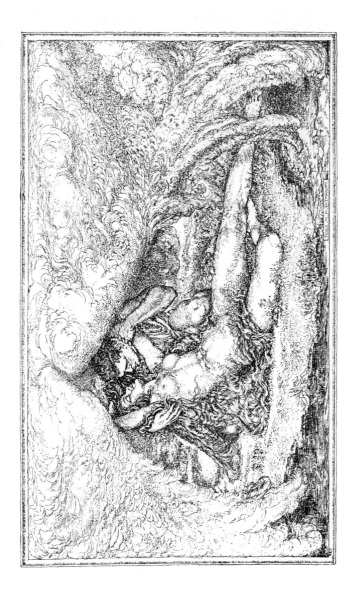

really seemed to me like a man, and as if it could speak."—As the waterfall came rushing down, it distinctly uttered these words in Huldbrand's ear :

> " Rash knight,
> Brave knight,
> Rage, feel I not,
> Chide, will I not.
> But ever guard thy little wife as well,
> Rash knight, brave knight ! Protect her well ! "

A few footsteps more, and they were upon open ground. The imperial city lay bright before them, and the evening sun, which gilded its towers, kindly dried the garments of the drenched wanderers.

HOW · THEY · LIVED · IN · THE · CITY

CHAPTER X.

HE sudden disappearance of the young knight, Huldbrand von Ringstetten, from the imperial city, had caused great sensation and solicitude among those who had admired him both for his skill in the tournament and the dance, and no less so for his gentle and agreeable manners. His servants would not quit the place without their master, although not one of them would have had the courage to go in quest of him into the shadowy recesses of the forest. They therefore remained in

108

their quarters, inactively hoping, as men are wont to do, and keeping alive the remembrance of their lost lord by their lamentations. When, soon after, the violent storms and floods were observed, the less doubt was entertained as to the certain destruction of the handsome stranger; and Bertalda openly mourned for him and blamed herself for having allured the unfortunate knight into the forest. Her foster-parents, the duke and duchess, had come to fetch her away, but Bertalda entreated them to remain with her until certain intelligence had been obtained of Huldbrand's fate. She endeavoured to prevail upon several young knights, who were eagerly courting her, to follow the noble adventurer to the forest. But she would not pledge her hand as the reward of the enterprise, because she always cherished the hope of belonging to the returning knight, and no glove, nor riband, nor even kiss, would tempt any one to expose his life for the sake of bringing back such a dangerous rival.

When Huldbrand now suddenly and unexpectedly appeared, his servants, and the inhabitants of the city, and almost every one, rejoiced. Bertalda alone refused to do so; for agreeable as it was to the others that he should bring with him such a beautiful bride, and Father Heilmann as a witness of the marriage, Bertalda could feel nothing but grief and vexation. In the first place, she had really loved the young knight with all her heart, and in the next, her sorrow at his absence had proclaimed this far more before the eyes of all, than was now befitting. She still however conducted herself as a wise maiden, reconciled herself to circumstances, and lived on the most friendly terms with Undine, who was looked upon throughout the city, as a princess, whom Huldbrand had rescued in the forest from some evil enchantment. When she or her husband were questioned on the matter, they were wise enough to be silent or skilfully to evade the inquiries. Father Heilmann's lips were sealed to idle gossip of any kind, and moreover, immediately after Huldbrand's arrival, he had returned to his monastery ; so that people were obliged to be satisfied with their own strange conjectures, and even Bertalda herself knew no more of the truth than others.

Day by day, Undine felt her affection increase for the fair maiden. "We must have known each other before," she often used to say to her, "or else, there must be some mysterious connection between us, for one does not love another as dearly as I have loved you from the first moment of our meeting, without some cause,—some deep and secret cause." And Bertalda also could not deny the fact that she felt drawn to Undine with a tender feeling of confidence, however much she might consider that she had cause for the bitterest lamentation at this successful rival. Biassed by this mutual affection, they both persuaded, —the one her foster-parents, the other her husband, —to postpone the day of departure from time to time ; indeed, it was even proposed that Bertalda should accompany Undine for a time to castle Ringstetten, near the source of the Danube.

They were talking over this plan one beautiful evening, as they were walking by starlight in the

large square of the Imperial city, under the tall trees
that enclose it. The young married pair had invited
Bertalda to join them in their evening walk, and all
three were strolling up and down under the dark blue
sky, often interrupting their familiar talk to admire
the magnificent fountain in the middle of the square,
as its waters rushed and bubbled forth with wonderful
beauty. It had a soothing, happy influence upon
them ; between the shadows of the trees, there stole
glimmerings of light from the adjacent houses ; a low
murmur of children at play, and of others enjoying
their walk, floated around them ; they were so alone,
and yet in the midst of the bright and living world ;
whatever had appeared difficult by day, now became
smooth as of itself ; and the three friends could no
longer understand why the slightest hesitation had
existed with regard to Bertalda's visit to Ringstetten.
Presently, just as they were on the point of fixing
the day for their common departure, a tall man
approached them from the middle of the square,
bowed respectfully to the company, and said
something in the ear of the young wife. Displeased
as she was at the interruption and its cause, she
stepped a little aside with the stranger, and both
began to whisper together, as it seemed, in a foreign
tongue. Huldbrand fancied he knew the strange
man, and he stared so fixedly at him, that he neither
heard nor answered Bertalda's astonished inquiries.
All at once, Undine clapped her hands joyfully, and,
laughing, quitted the stranger's side, who, shaking
his head, retired hastily and discontentedly, and
vanished in the fountain. Huldbrand now felt cer-

tain on the point, but Bertalda asked : " And what did the master of the fountain want with you, dear Undine ? " The young wife laughed within herself, and replied : " The day after to-morrow, my dear

child, on the anniversary of your name-day, you shall know it." And nothing more would she disclose. She invited Bertalda and sent an invitation to her foster-parents, to dine with them on the appointed day, and soon after they parted.

"Kühleborn ? was it Kühleborn ? " said Huldbrand,

with a secret shudder, to his beautiful bride, when they had taken leave of Bertalda, and were now going home through the darkening streets. "Yes, it was he," replied Undine; "and he was going to say all sorts of nonsensical things to me. But, in the midst, quite contrary to his intention, he delighted me with a most welcome piece of news. If you wish to hear it at once, my dear lord and husband, you have but to command, and I will tell it you without reserve. But if you would confer a real pleasure on your Undine, you will wait till the day after to-morrow, and you will then have your share too in the surprise."

The knight gladly complied with his wife's desire, which had been urged so sweetly, and as she fell asleep, she murmured smilingly to herself: "Dear, dear Bertalda! How she will rejoice and be astonished at what her master of the fountain told me!"

THE ANNIVERSARY OF BERTALDA'S NAME-DAY

CHAPTER XI

 HE company were sitting at dinner; Bertalda, looking like some goddess of spring with her flowers and jewels, the presents of her foster-parents and friends, was placed between Undine and Huldbrand. When the rich repast was ended, and the last course had appeared, the doors were left open, according to a good old German custom, that the common people might look on, and take part in the festivity of the nobles. Servants were carrying round cake and wine among the spectators. Huldbrand and Bertalda were waiting with secret impatience for the promised explanation, and sat with their eyes fixed steadily on

Undine. But the beautiful wife still continued silent, and only kept smiling to herself with secret and hearty satisfaction. All who knew of the promise she had given, could see that she was every moment on the point of betraying her happy secret, and that it was with a sort of a longing renunciation that she withheld it, just as children sometimes delay the enjoyment of their choicest morsels. Bertalda and Huldbrand shared this delightful feeling, and expected with fearful hope the tidings which were to fall from the lips of Undine. Several of the company pressed Undine to sing. The request seemed opportune, and ordering her lute to be brought, she sang the following words :

> Bright opening day,
> Wild flowers so gay,
> Tall grasses their thirst that slake,
> On the banks of the billowy lake !
> What glimmers there so shining
> The reedy growth entwining ?
> Is it a blossom white as snow
> Fallen from heav'n here below ?

> It is an infant, frail and dear !
> With flowerets playing in its dreams
> And grasping morning's golden beams ;—
> Oh ! whence, sweet stranger, art thou here ?
> From some far-off and unknown strand,
> The lake has borne thee to this land.

> Nay, grasp not, tender little one,
> With thy tiny hand outspread ;
> No hand will meet thy touch with love,
> Mute is that flowery bed.

The flowers can deck themselves so fair
And breathe forth fragrance blest,
Yet none can press thee to itself,
Like that far-off mother's breast.

So early at the gate of life,
With smiles of heav'n on thy brow,
Thou hast the best of treasures lost,
Poor wand'ring child, nor knows't it now.

A noble duke comes riding by,
And near thee checks his courser's speed,
And full of ardent chivalry
He bears thee home upon his steed.

Much, endless much, has been thy gain !
Thou bloom'st the fairest in the land !
Yet ah ! the priceless joy of all,
Thou'st left upon an unknown strand.

Undine dropped her lute with a melancholy smile, and the eyes of Bertalda's foster-parents were filled with tears. " Yes, so it was on the morning that I found you, my poor sweet orphan," said the duke deeply agitated ; "the beautiful singer is certainly right ; we have not been able to give you that ' priceless joy of all.' "

"But we must also hear how it fared with the poor parents," said Undine, as she resumed her lute, and sang :

Thro' every chamber roams the mother,
Moves and searches every where,
Seeks, she scarce knows what, with sadness,
And finds an empty house is there.

An empty house !   Oh word of sorrow,
To her who once had been so blest,
Who led her child about by day
And cradled it at night to rest.

The beech is growing green again,
The sunshine gilds its wonted spot,
But mother, cease thy searching vain !
Thy little loved one cometh not.

And when the breath of eve blows cool,
And father in his home appears,
The smile he almost tries to wear
Is quenched at once by gushing tears.

Full well he knows that in his home
He naught can find but wild despair,
He hears the mother's grieved lament
And no bright infant greets him there.

"Oh ! for God's sake, Undine, where are my parents?" cried the weeping Bertalda ; "you surely know, you have discovered them, you wonderful being, for otherwise you would not have thus torn my heart.   Are they perhaps already here?   Can it be?"   Her eye passed quickly over the brilliant company, and lingered on a lady of high rank who was sitting next her foster-father.   Undine however turned towards the door, while her eyes overflowed with the sweetest emotion.   "Where are the poor waiting parents?" she enquired, and the old fisher-man and his wife advanced hesitatingly from the crowd of spectators.   Their glance rested inquiringly, now on Undine, now on the beautiful girl who was said to be their daughter.   "It is she," said the delighted benefactress, in a faltering tone, and the two old people hung round the neck of their recovered child, weeping, and praising God.

But amazed and indignant, Bertalda tore herself from their embrace. Such a recognition was too much for this proud mind, at a moment when she had surely imagined that her former splendour would even be increased, and when hope was deluding her with a vision of almost royal honours. It seemed to her as if her rival had devised all this, on purpose signally to humble her before Huldbrand and the whole world. She reviled Undine, she reviled the old people, and bitter invectives, such as "deceiver" and "bribed impostors," fell from her lips. Then the old fisherman's wife said in a low voice to herself : "Ah me, she is become a wicked girl ; and yet I feel in my heart that she is my child." The old fisherman, however, had folded his hands, and was praying silently that this might not be his daughter. Undine, pale as death, turned with agitation from the parents to Bertalda, and from Bertalda to the parents ; suddenly cast down from that heaven of happiness of which she had dreamed, and overwhelmed with a fear and a terror such as she had never known even in imagination. "Have you a soul? Have you really a soul ? Bertalda ? " she cried again and again to her angry friend, as if forcibly to rouse her to consciousness from some sudden delirium or maddening nightmare. But when Bertalda only became more and more enraged, when the repulsed parents began to weep aloud, and the company, in eager dispute, were taking different sides, she begged in such a dignified and serious manner to be allowed to speak in this her husband's hall, that all around were in a moment silenced. She then advanced to the upper end of the table, where Bertalda had seated herself, and with a modest and yet proud air, while every eye was fixed upon her, she spoke as follows :

"My friends, you look so angry and disturbed, and you have interrupted my happy feast by your disputings. Ah ! I knew nothing of your foolish habits and your heartless mode of thinking, and I shall never all my life long become accustomed to them. It is not my fault that this affair has resulted in evil ; believe me, the fault is with yourselves alone, little as it may appear to you to be so. I have therefore but little to say to you, but one thing I must say : I have spoken nothing but truth. I neither can nor will give you proofs beyond my own assertion, but I will swear to the truth of this. I received this information from the very person who allured Bertalda into the water, away from her parents, and who afterwards placed her on the green meadow in the duke's path."

"She is an enchantress !" cried Bertalda, "a witch, who has intercourse with evil spirits. She acknowledges it herself."

" I do not," said Undine, with a whole heaven of innocence and confidence beaming in her eyes. "I am no witch ; only look at me ! "

"She is false and boastful," interrupted Bertalda, " and she cannot prove that I am the child of these low people. My noble parents, I beg you to take me from this company and out of this city, where

they are only bent on insulting me." But the aged
and honourable duke remained unmoved, and his
wife said : "We must thoroughly examine how we
are to act. God forbid that we should move a step

from this hall until we have done so." Then the
old wife of the fisherman drew near, and making a
low reverence to the duchess, she said : " Noble,
God-fearing lady, you have opened my heart. I
must tell you, if this evil-disposed young lady is my

123

daughter, she has a mark, like a violet, between her shoulders, and another like it on the instep of her left foot. If she would only go out of the hall with me!" "I shall not uncover myself before the peasant woman!" exclaimed Bertalda, proudly turning her back on her. "But before me you will," rejoined the duchess, very gravely. "Follow me into that room, girl, and the good old woman shall come with us." The three disappeared, and the rest of the company remained where they were, in silent expectation. After a short time they returned; Bertalda was pale as death. "Right is right," said the duchess; "I must therefore declare that our hostess has spoken perfect truth. Bertalda is the fisherman's daughter, and that is as much as it is necessary to inform you here." The princely pair left with their adopted daughter; and at a sign from the duke, the fisherman and his wife followed them. The other guests retired in silence or with secret murmurs, and Undine sank weeping into Huldbrand's arms.

HOW THEY LEFT THE IMPERIAL CITY

TO·SHARE·ALL·THINGS·AS·SISTERS:

CHAPTER XII

HE Lord of Ring-stetten would have certainly preferred the events of this day to have been different; but even as they were, he could scarcely regret them wholly, as they had exhibited his charming wife under such a good and sweet and kindly aspect. "If I have given her a soul," he could not help saying to himself, "I have indeed given her a better one than my own;" and his only thought now was to speak soothingly to the weeping Undine, and on the following morning, to quit with her a place which, after this incident, must have become distasteful to her. It is true that she was not esti-

127

mated differently to what she had been.. As something mysterious had long been expected of her, the strange discovery of Bertalda's origin had caused no great surprise, and every one who had heard the story and had seen Bertalda's violent behaviour, was disgusted with her alone. Of this, however, the knight and his lady knew nothing as yet; and, besides, the condemnation or approval of the public was equally painful to Undine, and thus there was no better course to pursue, than to leave the walls of the old city behind them with all the speed possible.

With the earliest beams of morning, a pretty carriage drove up to the entrance gate for Undine; the horses which Huldbrand and his squires were to ride, stood near, pawing the ground with impatient eagerness. The knight was leading his beautiful wife from the door, when a fisher-girl crossed their way. "We do not need your fish," said Huldbrand to her, "we are now starting on our journey." Upon this the fisher-girl began to weep bitterly, and the young couple perceived for the first time that it was Bertalda. They immediately returned with her to their apartment, and learned from her that the duke and duchess were so displeased at her violent and unfeeling conduct on the preceding day, that they had entirely withdrawn their protection from her though not without giving her a rich portion.

The fisherman, too, had been handsomely rewarded, and had the evening before set out with his wife to return to their secluded home.

"I would have gone with them," she continued,

"but the old fisherman, who is said to be my father—"

"And he is so indeed, Bertalda," interrupted Undine. "Mark me, the stranger, whom you took for the master of the fountain, told me the whole story in detail. He wished to dissuade me from taking you with me to castle Ringstetten, and this led him to disclose the secret."

"Well then," said Bertalda—"if it must be so, —my father said : 'I will not take you with me until you are changed. Venture to come to us alone through the haunted forest ; that shall be the proof whether you have any regard for us. But do not come to me as a lady ; come only as a fisher-girl !' So I will do just as he has told me, for I am forsaken by the whole world, and I will live and die in solitude as a poor fisher-girl, with my poor parents. I have a terrible dread though of the forest. Horrible spectres are said to dwell in it, and I am so fearful. But how can I help it? I only came here to implore pardon of the noble lady of Ringstetten for my unbecoming behaviour yesterday. I feel sure, sweet lady, you meant to do me a kindness, but you knew not how you would wound me, and in my agony and surprise, many a rash and frantic expression passed my lips. Oh forgive, forgive ! I am already so unhappy. Only think yourself what I was yesterday morning, yesterday at the beginning of your banquet, and what I am now !"

Her voice became stifled with a passionate flood of tears, and Undine, also weeping bitterly, fell on her neck. It was some time before the deeply agitated Undine could utter a word ; at length she said :

"You can go with us to Ringstetten ; everything shall remain as it was arranged before ; only do not speak to me again as 'noble lady.' You see, we were exchanged for each other as children ; our faces even then sprang as it were from the same stem, and we will now so strengthen this kindred destiny that no human power shall be able to separate it. Only, first of all, come with us to Ringstetten. We will discuss there, how we will share all things as sisters." Bertalda looked timidly towards Huldbrand. He pitied the beautiful girl in her distress, and offering her his hand, he begged her tenderly to entrust herself with him and his wife. "We will send a message to your parents," he continued, "to tell them why you are not come ; " and he would have added more with regard to the worthy fisherman and his wife, but he saw that Bertalda shrank with pain from the mention of their name, and he therefore refrained from saying more.

He then assisted her first into the carriage, Undine followed her ; and he mounted his horse and trotted merrily by the side of them, urging the driver at the same time to hasten his speed, so that very soon they were beyond the confines of the Imperial city and all its sad remembrances ; and now the ladies began to enjoy the beautiful country through which their road lay.

After a journey of some days, they arrived one exquisite evening, at castle Ringstetten. The young knight had much to hear from his overseers and vassals, so that Undine and Bertalda were left alone.

They both repaired to the ramparts of the fortress, and were delighted with the beautiful landscape which spread far and wide through fertile Swabia.

Presently a tall man approached them, greeting them respectfully, and Bertalda fancied she saw a resemblance to the master of the fountain in the Imperial city. Still more unmistakable grew the likeness, when Undine angrily and almost threateningly waved him off, and he retreated with hasty steps and shaking head, as he had done before, and disappeared into a neighbouring copse. Undine, however, said : " Don't be afraid, dear Bertalda, this time the hateful master of the fountain shall do you no harm." And then she told her the whole story in detail, and who she was herself, and how Bertalda had been taken away from the fisherman and his wife, and Undine had gone to them. The girl was at first terrified with this relation ; she imagined her friend must be seized with sudden madness, but she became more convinced that all was true, for Undine's story was so connected, and fitted so well with former occurrences, and still more she had that inward feeling with which truth never fails to make itself known to us. It seemed strange to her that she was now herself living, as it were, in the midst of one of those fairy tales to which she had formerly only listened.

She gazed upon Undine with reverence, but she could not resist a sense of dread that seemed to come between her and her friend, and at their evening repast she could not but wonder, how the knight could behave so lovingly and kindly towards a being who appeared to her, since the discovery she had just made, more of a phantom than a human being.

HOW THEY LIVED AT CASTLE
RINGSTETTEN

CHAPTER XIII

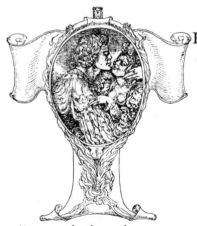

HE writer of this story, both because it moves his own heart, and because he wishes it to move that of others, begs you, dear reader, to pardon him, if he now briefly passes over a considerable space of time, only cursorily mentioning the events that marked it. He knows well that he might portray skilfully, step by step, how Huldbrand's heart began to turn from Undine to Bertalda; how Bertalda more and more responded with ardent affection to the young knight, and how they both looked upon the poor wife as a

135

mysterious being rather to be feared than pitied ;
how Undine wept, and how her tears stung the
knight's heart with remorse without awakening his
former love, so that though he at times was kind and
endearing to her, a cold shudder would soon draw
him from her, and he would turn to his fellow-mortal,
Bertalda. All this the reader knows might be fully
detailed, and perhaps ought to have been so ; but
such a task would have been too painful, for similar
things have been known to him by sad experience, and
he shrinks from their shadow even in remembrance.
You know probably a like feeling, dear reader, for
such is the lot of mortal man. Happy are you if
you have received rather than inflicted the pain, for
in such things it is more blessed to receive than to
give. If it be so, such recollections will only bring
a feeling of sorrow to your mind, and perhaps a tear
will trickle down your cheek over the faded flowers
that once caused you such delight. But let that be
enough. We will not pierce our hearts with a
thousand separate things, but only briefly state, as I
have just said, how matters were.

Poor Undine was very sad, and the other two
were not to be called happy. Bertalda especially
thought that she could trace the effect of jealousy on
the part of the injured wife whenever her wishes were
in any way thwarted by her. She had therefore
habituated herself to an imperious demeanour, to which
Undine yielded in sorrowful submission, and the now
blinded Huldbrand usually encouraged this arrogant
behaviour in the strongest manner. But the circumstance that most of all disturbed the inmates of the

IT IS MORE BLESSED TO

LORD JESUS SAID IT IS

RECEIVE THAN TO GIVE

castle, was a variety of wonderful apparitions which met Huldbrand and Bertalda in the vaulted galleries of the castle, and which had never been heard of before as haunting the locality. The tall white man, in whom Huldbrand recognized only too plainly uncle Kühleborn, and Bertalda the spectral master of the fountain, often passed before them with a threatening aspect, and especially before Bertalda ; so much so, that she had already several times been made ill with terror, and had frequently thought of quitting the castle. But still she stayed there, partly because Huldbrand was so dear to her, and she relied on her innocence, no words of love having ever passed between them, and partly also because she knew not whither to direct her steps. The old fisherman, on receiving the message from the lord of Ringstetten that Bertalda was his guest, had written a few lines in an almost illegible hand, but as good as his advanced age and long disuse would admit of. " I have now become," he wrote, " a poor old widower, for my dear and faithful wife is dead. However lonely I now sit in my cottage, Bertalda is better with you than with me. Only let her do nothing to harm my beloved Undine ! She will have my curse if it be so." The last words of this letter, Bertalda flung to the winds, but she carefully retained the part respecting her absence from her father,—just as we are all wont to do in similar circumstances.

One day, when Huldbrand had just ridden out, Undine summoned together the domestics of the family, and ordered them to bring a large stone, and carefully to cover with it the magnificent fountain

139

which stood in the middle of the castle-yard. The servants objected that it would oblige them to bring water from the valley below. Undine smiled sadly. "I am sorry, my people," she replied, "to increase your work. I would rather myself fetch up the pitchers, but this fountain must be closed. Believe me that it cannot be otherwise, and that it is only by so doing that we can avoid a greater evil."

The whole household were glad to be able to please their gentle mistress; they made no further enquiry, but seized the enormous stone. They were just raising it in their hands, and were already poising it over the fountain, when Bertalda came running up, and called out to them to stop, as it was from this fountain that the water was brought which was so good for her complexion, and she would never consent to its being closed. Undine, however, although gentle as usual, was more than usually firm. She told Bertalda that it was her due, as mistress of the house, to arrange her household as she thought best, and that, in this, she was accountable to no one but her lord and husband. "See, oh, pray see," exclaimed Bertalda, in an angry yet uneasy tone, "how the poor beautiful water is curling and writhing at being shut out from the bright sunshine and from the cheerful sight of the human face, for whose mirror it was created!" The water in the fountain was indeed wonderfully agitated and hissing; it seemed as if something within were struggling to free itself, but Undine only the more earnestly urged the fulfilment of her orders. The earnestness was scarcely needed. The servants of the castle were as happy in obeying their gentle mistress as in opposing Bertalda's haughty defiance ; and in spite of all the rude scolding and threatening of the latter, the stone was soon firmly lying over the opening of the fountain. Undine leaned thoughtfully over it, and wrote with her beautiful fingers on its surface. She must, however, have had something very sharp and cutting in her hand, for when she turned away, and the servants drew near to examine the stone, they perceived various strange characters upon it, which none of them had seen there before.

Bertalda received the knight on his return home in the evening, with tears and complaints of Undine's conduct. He cast a serious look at his poor wife, and she looked down as if distressed. Yet she said with great composure : " My lord and husband does not reprove even a bondslave without a hearing, how much less, then, his wedded wife ? " " Speak," said the knight with a gloomy countenance, " what induced you to act so strangely ? " " I should like to tell you when we are quite alone," sighed Undine. " You can tell me just as well in Bertalda's presence," was the rejoinder. " Yes, if you command me," said Undine; " but command it not. Oh pray, pray command it not ! " She looked so humble, so sweet, and obedient, that the knight's heart felt a passing gleam from better times. He kindly placed her arm within his own, and led her to his apartment, when she began to speak as follows :

" You already know, my beloved lord, something of my evil uncle, Kühleborn, and you have frequently been displeased at meeting him in the galleries of this

141

castle. He has several time frightened Bertalda into illness. This is because he is devoid of soul, a mere elemental mirror of the outward world, without the power of reflecting the world within. He sees, too, sometimes, that you are dissatisfied with me ; that I, in my childishness, am weeping at this, and that Bertalda perhaps is at the very same moment laughing. Hence he imagines various discrepancies in our home life, and in many ways mixes unbidden with our circle. What is the good of reproving him? What is the use of sending him angrily away? He does not believe a word I say. His poor nature has no idea that the joys and sorrows of love have so sweet a resemblance, and are so closely linked that no power can separate them. Amid tears a smile shines forth, and a smile allures tears from their secret chambers."

She looked up at Huldbrand, smiling and weeping; and he again experienced within his heart all the charm of his old love. She felt this, and pressing him more tenderly to her, she continued amid tears of joy : "As the disturber of our peace was not to be dismissed with words, I have been obliged to shut the door upon him. And the only door by which he obtains access to us, is that fountain. He is cut off by the adjacent valleys from the other water-spirits in the neighbourhood, and his kingdom only commences further off on the Danube, into which some of his good friends direct their course. For this reason, I had the stone placed over the opening of the fountain, and I inscribed characters upon it which cripple all my uncle's power, so that he can now neither intrude upon you, nor upon me, nor upon Bertalda. Human beings, it is true, can raise the stone again with ordinary effort, in spite of the characters inscribed on it. The inscription does not hinder them. If you wish, therefore, follow Bertalda's desire, but, truly! she knows not what she asks. The rude Kühleborn has set his mark especially upon her; and if much came to pass which he has predicted to me, and which might indeed happen without your meaning any evil,—ah! dear one, even you would then be exposed to danger!"

Huldbrand felt deeply the generosity of his sweet wife, in her eagerness to shut up her formidable protector, while she had even been chided for it by Bertalda. He pressed her in his arms with the utmost affection, and said with emotion : "The stone shall remain, and all shall remain, now and ever, as you wish to have it, my sweet Undine." She caressed him with humble delight as she heard the expressions of love so long withheld, and then at length she said: "My dearest husband, you are so gentle and kind to-day, may I venture to ask a favour of you? See now, it is just the same with you as it is with summer. In the height of its glory, summer puts on the flaming and thundering crown of mighty storms, and assumes the air of a king over the earth. You too, sometimes, let your fury rise, and your eyes flash and your voice is angry, and this becomes you well, though I in my folly may sometimes weep at it. But never, I pray you, behave thus towards me on the water, or even when we are near it. You see, my relatives would then acquire a right over me. They would unrelentingly tear me from you in their rage ; because they would imagine that one of their race was injured, and

I should be compelled all my life to dwell below in the crystal palaces, and should never dare to ascend to you again ; or they would send me up to you,— and that, oh God, would be infinitely worse. No, no, my beloved husband, do not let it come to that, if your poor Undine is dear to you."

He promised solemnly to do as she desired, and they both returned from the apartment, full of happiness and affection. At that moment Bertalda appeared with some workmen, to whom she had already given orders, and said in a sullen tone, which she had assumed of late : " I suppose the secret conference is at an end, and now the stone may be removed. Go out, workmen, and attend to it." But the knight, angry at her impertinence, desired, in short and very decisive words, that the stone should be left ; he reproved Bertalda, too, for her violence towards his wife. Whereupon the workmen withdrew, smiling with secret satisfaction ; while Bertalda, pale with rage, hurried away to her room.

The hour for the evening repast arrived, and Bertalda was waited for in vain. They sent after her, but the domestic found her apartments empty, and only brought back with him a sealed letter addressed to the knight. He opened it with alarm, and read : " I feel with shame that I am only a poor fisher-girl. I will expiate my fault in having forgotten this for a moment, by going to the miserable cottage of my parents. Farewell to you, and your beautiful wife."

Undine was heartily distressed. She earnestly entreated Huldbrand to hasten after their friend and

bring her back again. Alas ! she had no need to
urge him. His affection for Bertalda burst forth
again with vehemence. He hurried round the castle,
enquiring if any one had seen which way the fugitive

*" How Undine wept, and how her tears stung the Knight's heart with
remorse without awakening his former love."*

had gone. He could learn nothing of her, and he
was already on his horse in the castle-yard, resolved
at a venture to take the road by which he had
brought Bertalda hither. Just then a page appeared,
145   L

who assured him that he had met the lady on the path to the Black Valley. Like an arrow, the knight sprang through the gateway in the direction indicated, without hearing Undine's voice of agony, as she called to him from the window : "To the Black Valley ! Oh, not there ! Huldbrand, don't go there ! or, for Heaven's sake, take me with you !" But when she perceived that all her calling was in vain, she ordered her white palfrey to be immediately saddled, and rode after the knight, without allowing any servant to accompany her.

CHAPTER XIV

HE Black Valley lies deep within the mountains. What it is now called, we do not know. At that time the people of the country gave it this appellation on account of the deep obscurity in which the low land lay, owing to the shadows of the lofty trees, and especially firs, that grew there. Even the brook which bubbled between the rocks wore the same dark hue, and dashed along with none of that gladness with which streams are wont to flow that have the blue sky immediately above them. Now, in the growing twilight of evening, it looked wild and gloomy between the heights. The knight trotted anxiously along the edge of the brook, fearful at one moment that by delay he might allow the fugitive to advance too far, and at the next, that by too great rapidity he might overlook her in case she were concealing herself from him. Meanwhile he had already penetrated tolerably far into the valley, and might soon hope to overtake the maiden, if he were on the right track. The fear that this might not be the case, made his heart beat with anxiety. Where would the tender Bertalda tarry through the stormy night, which was so fearful in the valley, should he fail to find her? At length he saw something white gleaming through the branches on the slope of the mountain. He thought he recognised Bertalda's dress, and he turned his course in that direction. But his horse refused to go forward; it reared impatiently; and its master, unwilling to lose a moment, and seeing moreover that the copse was impassable on horseback, dismounted; and, fastening his snorting steed to an elm-tree, he worked his way cautiously through the bushes. The branches sprinkled his forehead and cheeks with the cold drops of the evening dew; a distant roll of thunder was heard murmuring from the other side of the mountains; everything looked so strange, that he began to feel a dread of the white figure, which now lay only a short distance from him on the ground. Still he could plainly see that it was a female, either asleep or in a swoon, and that she was attired in long white garments, such as Bertalda had worn on that day. He stepped close up to her, made a rustling with the branches, and let his sword clatter, but she moved not. "Bertalda!" he exclaimed, at first in a low voice, and then louder and louder,—still she heard not. At last, when he uttered the dear name with a more powerful effort, a hollow echo from the mountain-caverns of the valley indistinctly reverberated "Bertalda!" but still the sleeper woke not. He bent down over her; the gloom of the valley and the obscurity of approaching night would not allow him to distinguish her features. Just as he was stooping closer over her, with a feeling of painful doubt, a flash of lightning shot across the valley, and he saw before him a frightfully distorted countenance, and a hollow voice exclaimed : "Give me a kiss, you enamoured swain!" Huldbrand sprang up with a cry of horror, and the hideous figure rose with him. "Go home!" it murmured; "wizards are on the watch. Go home! or I will have you!" and it stretched out its long white arms towards him. "Malicious Kühleborn!" cried the knight, recovering himself, "What do you concern me, you goblin? There, take your kiss!" And he furiously hurled his sword at the figure. But it vanished like vapour, and a gush of water which wetted him through, left the knight no doubt as to the foe with whom he had been engaged.

"He wishes to frighten me back from Bertalda," said he aloud to himself; "he thinks to terrify me with his foolish tricks, and to make me give up the poor distressed girl to him, so that he can wreak his vengeance on her. But he shall not do that, weak spirit of the elements, as he is. No powerless phantom can understand what a human heart can do when its best energies are aroused." He felt the truth of his words, and that the very expression of them had inspired his heart with fresh courage. It seemed too as if fortune were on his side, for he had not reached his fastened horse, when he distinctly heard Bertalda's plaintive voice not far distant, and could catch her weeping accents through the ever increasing tumult of the thunder and tempest. He hurried swiftly in the direction of the sound, and found the trembling girl just attempting to climb the steep, in order to escape in any way from the dreadful gloom of the valley. He stepped, however, lovingly in her path, and bold and proud as her resolve had before been, she now felt only too keenly the delight, that the friend whom she so passionately loved should rescue her from this frightful solitude, and that the joyous life in the castle should be again open to her. She followed almost unresisting, but so exhausted with fatigue that the knight was glad to have brought her to his horse, which he now hastily unfastened, in order to lift the fair fugitive upon it; and then, cautiously holding the reins, he hoped to proceed through the uncertain shades of the valley.

But the horse had become quite unmanageable from the wild apparition of Kühleborn. Even the knight would have had difficulty in mounting the rearing and snorting animal, but to place the trembling Bertalda on its back was perfectly impossible. They determined therefore to return home on foot. Drawing the horse after him by the bridle, the knight supported the tottering girl with his other hand. Bertalda exerted all her strength to pass quickly through the fearful valley, but weariness weighed her down like lead, and every limb trembled, partly from the terror she had endured when Kühleborn had pursued her, and partly from her continued alarm at the howling of the storm and the pealing of the thunder through the wooded mountain.

At last she slided from the supporting arm of her protector, and sinking down on the moss, she exclaimed : " Let me die here, my noble lord ; I suffer the punishment due to my folly, and I must now perish here through weariness and dread." " No, sweet friend, I will never leave you !" cried Huldbrand, vainly endeavouring to restrain his furious steed ; for, worse than before, it now began to foam and rear with excitement, till at last the knight was glad to keep the animal at a sufficient distance from the exhausted maiden, lest her fears should be increased. But scarcely had he withdrawn a few paces with the wild steed, than she began to call after him in the most pitiful manner, believing that he was really going to leave her in this horrible wilderness. He was utterly at a loss what course to take. Gladly would he have given the excited beast its liberty and have allowed it to rush away into the night and spend its fury, had he not feared that in this narrow defile it might come thundering with its iron-shod hoofs over the very spot where Bertalda lay.

In the midst of this extreme perplexity and distress, he heard with delight the sound of a vehicle driving slowly down the stony road behind them. He called out for help ; and a man's voice replied, bidding him have patience, but promising assistance ; and soon after, two grey horses appeared through the bushes, and beside them the driver in the white smock of a carter ; a great white linen cloth was next visible, covering the goods apparently contained in the waggon. At a loud shout from their master, the obedient horses halted. The driver then came towards the knight, and helped him in restraining his foaming animal. " I see well," said he, " what ails the beast. When I first travelled this way, my horses were no better. The fact is, there is an evil water-spirit haunting the place, and he takes delight in this sort of mischief. But I have learned a charm ; if you will let me whisper it in your horse's ear, he will stand at once just as quiet as my grey beasts are doing there." " Try your luck then, only help us quickly !" exclaimed the impatient knight. The waggoner then drew down the head of the rearing charger close to his own, and whispered something in his ear. In a moment the animal stood still and quiet, and his quick panting and reeking condition was all that remained of his previous unmanageable-ness. Huldbrand had no time to enquire how all this had been effected. He agreed with the carter that he should take Bertalda on his waggon, where, as the man assured him, there were a quantity of soft cotton bales, upon which she could be conveyed to castle Ringstetten, and the knight was to accompany them on horseback. But the horse appeared too much exhausted by its past fury to be able to carry his master so far, so the carter persuaded Huldbrand to get into the waggon with Bertalda. The horse could be fastened on behind. "We are going down hill," said he, "and that will make it light for my grey beasts."

The knight accepted the offer and entered the waggon with Bertalda ; the horse followed patiently behind, and the waggoner, steady and attentive, walked by the side.

In the stillness of the night, as its darkness deepened and the subsiding tempest sounded more and more remote, encouraged by the sense of security and their fortunate escape, a confidential conversation arose between Huldbrand and Bertalda. With flattering words he reproached her for her daring flight ; she excused herself with humility and emotion, and from every word she said, a gleam shone forth which disclosed distinctly to the lover, that the beloved was his. The knight felt the sense of her words far more than he regarded their meaning, and it was the sense alone to which he replied. Presently the waggoner suddenly shouted with a loud voice : "Up, my greys, up with your feet, keep together ! remember who you are !" The knight leaned out of the waggon and saw that the horses were stepping into the midst of a foaming stream or were already almost swimming, while the wheels of the waggon were rushing round and gleaming like mill-wheels, and the waggoner had got up in front, in consequence of the increasing waters. "What sort of a road is this ? It goes into the very middle of the stream," cried Huldbrand to his guide. "Not at all, sir," returned the other laughing, "it is just the reverse, the stream goes into the very middle of our road. Look round and see how every thing is covered by the water."

The whole valley indeed was suddenly filled with the surging flood, that visibly increased. " It is Kühleborn, the evil water-spirit, who wishes to drown us ! " exclaimed the knight. " Have you no charm against him, my friend ? "

" I know indeed of one," returned the waggoner, " but I cannot and may not use it until you know who I am."

" Is this a time for riddles ? " cried the knight. " The flood is ever rising higher, and what does it matter to me to know who you are ? " " It does matter to you though," said the waggoner, " for I am Kühleborn."

So saying, he thrust his distorted face into the waggon with a grin, but the waggon was a waggon no longer, the horses were not horses—all was transformed to foam and vanished in the hissing waves, and even the waggoner himself, rising as a gigantic billow, drew down the vainly struggling horse beneath the waters, and then swelling higher and higher, swept over the heads of the floating pair, like some liquid tower, threatening to bury them irrecoverably.

Just then the soft voice of Undine sounded through the uproar, the moon emerged from the clouds, and by its light Undine was seen on the heights above the valley. She rebuked, she threatened the floods below ; the menacing tower-like wave vanished, muttering and murmuring, the waters flowed gently away in the moonlight, and like a

white dove, Undine flew down from the height, seized the knight and Bertalda, and bore them with her to a fresh green turfy spot on the hill, where with choice refreshing restoratives, she dispelled their terrors and weariness ; then she assisted Bertalda to mount the white palfrey, on which she had herself ridden here, and thus all three returned back to castle Ringstetten.

THE JOURNEY TO VIENNA

CHAPTER. 15.

CHAPTER XV

THE JOURNEY TO VIENNA

"*In the newly-awakened love and esteem of her husband, many a gleam of hope and joy shone upon her.*"

FTER this last adventure, they lived quietly and happily at the castle. The knight more and more perceived the heavenly goodness of his wife, which had been so nobly exhibited by her pursuit, and by her rescue of them in the Black Valley, where Kühleborn's power again commenced ; Undine herself felt that peace and security which is never lacking to a mind, so long as it is distinctly conscious of being on the right path, and besides, in the newly-awakened love and esteem of her husband, many a gleam of hope and joy shone upon her. Bertalda, on the other hand, shewed herself grateful, humble, and timid, without regarding her conduct as anything meritorious. Whenever Huldbrand or Undine were about to give her any explanation regarding the covering of the fountain or the adventure in the Black Valley, she would earnestly entreat them to spare her the recital, as she felt too much shame at the recollection of the fountain, and too much fear at the remembrance of the Black Valley. She learned therefore nothing further of either ; and for what end was such knowledge necessary ? Peace and joy had visibly taken up their abode at castle Ringstetten. They felt secure on this point, and imagined that life could now produce nothing but pleasant flowers and fruits.

In this happy condition of things, winter had come and passed away, and spring with its fresh green shoots and its blue sky, was gladdening the joyous inmates of the castle. Spring was in harmony with them, and they with spring. What wonder, then, that its storks and swallows inspired them also with a desire to travel ? One day when they were taking a pleasant walk to one of the sources of the Danube, Huldbrand spoke of the magnificence of the noble river, and how it widened as it flowed through countries fertilized by its waters, how the charming city of Vienna shone forth on its banks, and how with every step of its course it increased in power and loveliness. " It must be glorious to go down the river as far as Vienna ! " exclaimed Bertalda, but immediately relapsing into her present modesty and humility, she paused and blushed deeply. This touched Undine deeply, and with the liveliest desire to give pleasure to her friend, she said : " What hinders us from starting on the little voyage ? " Bertalda exhibited the greatest delight, and both she and Undine began at once to picture the tour of the Danube in the brightest colours. Huldbrand also gladly agreed to the prospect ; only he once whispered anxiously in Undine's ear : " But Kühleborn becomes possessed of his power again out there ! " " Let him come," she replied with a smile, " I shall be there, and he ventures upon none of his mischief before me." The last impediment was thus removed ; they prepared for the journey, and soon after set out upon it with fresh spirits and the brightest hopes.

But wonder not, oh man, if events always turn out different to what we have intended. That malicious power, lurking for our destruction, gladly lulls its chosen victim to sleep with sweet songs and golden delusions ; while on the other hand the rescuing messenger from Heaven often knocks sharply and alarmingly at our door.

During the first few days of their voyage down the Danube, they were extremely happy. Everything grew more and more beautiful, as they sailed further and further down the proudly flowing stream. But in a region, otherwise so pleasant, and in the enjoyment of which they had promised themselves the purest delight, the ungovernable Kühleborn began, undisguisedly, to exhibit his power of interference. This was indeed manifested in mere teasing tricks, for Undine often rebuked the agitated waves, or the contrary winds, and then the violence of the enemy would be immediately humbled ; but again the attacks would be renewed, and again Undine's reproofs would become necessary, so that the pleasure of the little party was completely destroyed. The boatmen too were continually whispering to each other in dismay, and looking with distrust at the three strangers, whose servants even began more and more to forebode something uncomfortable, and to watch their superiors with suspicious glances. Huldbrand often said to himself : " This comes from like not being linked with like, from a man uniting himself with a mermaid ! " Excusing himself as we all love to do, he would often think indeed as he said this : " I did not really know that she was a sea-maiden, mine is the misfortune, that every step I take is disturbed and haunted by the wild caprices of her race, but mine is not the fault." By thoughts such as these, he felt himself in some measure strengthened, but on the other hand, he felt increasing ill humour, and almost animosity towards Undine. He would look at her with an expression of anger, the meaning of which the poor wife understood well. Wearied with this exhibition of displeasure, and exhausted by the constant effort to frustrate Kühleborn's artifices, she sank one evening into a deep slumber, rocked soothingly by the softly gliding bark.

Scarcely however had she closed her eyes, than every one in the vessel imagined he saw, in whatever direction he turned, a most horrible human head ; it rose out of the waves, not like that of a person swimming, but perfectly perpendicular as if invisibly supported upright on the watery surface, and floating along in the same course with the bark. Each wanted to point out to the other the cause of his alarm, but each found the same expression of horror depicted on the face of his neighbour, only that his hands and eyes were directed to a different point where the monster, half laughing and half threatening, rose before him. When, however, they all wished to make each other understand what each saw, and all were crying out : "Look there—! No, —there !" the horrible heads all at one and the same time appeared to their view, and the whole river around the vessel swarmed with the most hideous apparitions. The universal cry raised at the sight awoke Undine. As she opened her eyes, the wild crowd of distorted visages disappeared. But Huldbrand was indignant at such unsightly jugglery. He would have burst forth in uncontrolled imprecations, had not Undine said to him with a humble manner and a softly imploring tone : "For God's sake, my husband, we are on the water, do not be angry with me now." The knight was silent, and sat down absorbed in reverie. Undine whispered in his ear: "Would it not be better, my love, if we gave up this foolish journey, and returned to castle Ringstetten in peace?" But Huldbrand murmured moodily: "So I must be a prisoner in my own castle, and only be able to breathe so long as the fountain is closed! I would your mad kindred—" Undine lovingly pressed her fair hand upon his lips. He paused, pondering in silence over much that Undine had before said to him.

Bertalda had meanwhile given herself up to a variety of strange thoughts. She knew a good deal of Undine's origin, and yet not the whole, and the fearful Kühleborn especially had remained to her a terrible but wholly unrevealed mystery. She had indeed never even heard his name. Musing on these strange things, she unclasped, scarcely conscious of the act, a gold necklace, which Huldbrand had lately purchased for her of a travelling trader; half dreamingly she drew it along the surface of the water, enjoying the light glimmer it cast upon the evening-tinted stream. Suddenly a huge hand was stretched out of the Danube, it seized the necklace and vanished with it beneath the waters. Bertalda screamed aloud, and a scornful laugh resounded from the depths of the stream. The knight could now restrain his anger no longer. Starting up, he inveighed against the river; he cursed all who ventured to interfere with his family and his life, and challenged them, be they spirits or sirens, to show themselves before his avenging sword.

Bertalda wept meanwhile for her lost ornament, which was so precious to her, and her tears added fuel

to the flame of the knight's anger, while Undine held
her hand over the side of the vessel, dipping it into
the water, softly murmuring to herself, and only now
and then interrupting her strange mysterious whisper,
as she entreated her husband : " My dearly loved one,
do not scold me here ; reprove others if you will,
but not me here. You know why ! " And, indeed,
he restrained the words of anger that were trembling
on his tongue. Presently in her wet hand which she
had been holding under the waves, she brought up a
beautiful coral necklace of so much brilliancy that
the eyes of all were dazzled by it. " Take this,"
said she, holding it out kindly to Bertalda ; " I have
ordered this to be brought for you as a compensation,
and don't be grieved any more, my poor child."
But the knight sprang between them. He tore the
beautiful ornament from Undine's hand, hurled it
again into the river, exclaiming in passionate rage :
" Have you then still a connection with them ? In
the name of all the witches, remain among them with
your presents, and leave us mortals in peace, you
sorceress ! " Poor Undine gazed at him with fixed
but tearful eyes, her hand still stretched out, as when
she had offered her beautiful present so lovingly to
Bertalda. She then began to weep more and more
violently, like a dear innocent child, bitterly afflicted.
At last, wearied out, she said : " Alas, sweet friend,
alas ! farewell ! They shall do you no harm ; only
remain true, so that I may be able to keep them
from you. I must, alas, go away ; I must go hence
at this early stage of life. Oh woe, woe ; what have
you done ! Oh woe, woe ! "

She vanished over the side of the vessel. Whether she plunged into the stream, or flowed away with it, they knew not ; her disappearance was like both and neither. Soon, however, she was completely lost sight of in the Danube ; only a few little waves kept whispering, as if sobbing, round the boat, and they almost seemed to be saying : "Oh woe, woe ! oh remain true ! oh woe !"

Huldbrand lay on the deck of the vessel, bathed in hot tears, and a deep swoon soon cast its veil of forgetfulness over the unhappy man.

CHAPTER XVI

HOW IT FARED FURTHER WITH HULDBRAND

"FAIL-NOT MY TOTTERING FRAME,
TILL YOU HAVE REACHED
THE GOAL!"

HALL we say it is well or ill, that our sorrow is of such short duration? I mean that deep sorrow which affects the very well-spring of our life, which becomes so one with the lost objects of our love that they are no longer lost, and which enshrines their image as a sacred treasure, until that final goal is reached which they have reached before us! It is true that many men really maintain these sacred memories, but their feeling is no longer that of the first deep grief. Other and new images have thronged between; we learn at length the transitoriness of all earthly things, even to our grief, and therefore I must say "Alas, that our sorrow should be of such short duration!"

The lord of Ringstetten experienced this: whether for his good, we shall hear in the sequel to this history. At first he could do nothing but weep, and that as bitterly as the poor gentle Undine had wept, when he had torn from her hand that brilliant ornament with which she had wished to set everything to rights. And then he would stretch out his hand, as she had done, and would weep again, like her. He cherished the secret hope that he might at length dissolve in tears; and has not a similar hope passed before the mind of many a one of us, with painful pleasure, in moments of great affliction? Bertalda wept also, and they lived a long while quietly together at castle Ringstetten, cherishing Undine's memory, and almost wholly forgetful of their former attachment to each other. And therefore the good Undine often visited Huldbrand in his dreams; caressing him tenderly and kindly, and then going away, weeping silently, so that when he awoke he often scarcely knew why his cheeks were so wet: whether they had been bathed with her tears, or merely with his own!

These dream-visions became however less frequent as time passed on, and the grief of the knight was less acute; still he would probably have cherished no other wish than thus to think calmly of Undine and to talk of her, had not the old fisherman appeared one day unexpectedly at the castle, and sternly insisted on Bertalda's returning with him as his child. The news of Undine's disappearance had reached him, and he had determined on no longer allowing Bertalda to reside at the castle with the widowed knight. "For," said he, "whether my daughter loves me or not, I do not care to know, but her honour is at stake, and where that is concerned, nothing else is to be thought of."

This idea of the old fisherman's, and the solitude which threatened to overwhelm the knight in all the halls and galleries of the desolate castle, after Bertalda's departure, brought out the feelings that had slumbered till now and which had been wholly forgotten in his sorrow for Undine;—namely, Huldbrand's affection for the beautiful Bertalda. The fisherman had many objections to raise against the proposed marriage. Undine had been very dear to the old fisherman, and he felt that no one really knew for certain whether the dear lost one were actually dead. And if her body were truly lying cold and stiff at the bottom of the Danube, or had floated away with the current into the ocean, even then, Bertalda was in some measure to blame for her death, and it was unfitting for her to step into the place of the poor supplanted one. Yet the fisherman had a strong regard for the knight also; and the entreaties of his daughter, who had become much more gentle and submissive, and her tears for Undine, turned the scale, and he must at length have given his consent, for he remained at the castle without objection, and a messenger was despatched to Father Heilmann, who had united Undine and Huldbrand in happy days gone by, to bring him to the castle for the second nuptials of the knight.

The holy man, however, had scarcely read the letter from the knight of Ringstetten, than he set out on his journey to the castle, with far greater expedition than even the messenger had used in going to him. Whenever his breath failed in his rapid progress, or his aged limbs ached with weariness, he would say to himself : " Perhaps the evil may yet be prevented ; fail not, my tottering frame, till you have reached the goal ! " And with renewed power he would then press forward, and go on and on without rest or repose, until late one evening he entered the shady court-yard of castle Ringstetten.

The betrothed pair were sitting side by side under the trees, and the old fisherman was near them, absorbed in thought. The moment they recognised Father Heilmann, they sprang up, and pressed round him with warm welcome. But he, without making much reply, begged Huldbrand to go with him into the castle ; and when the latter looked astonished, and hesitated to obey the grave summons, the reverend father said to him : " Why should I make any delay in wishing to speak to you in private, Herr von Ringstetten ? What I have to say concerns Bertalda and the fisherman as much as yourself, and what a man has to hear, he may prefer to hear as soon as possible. Are you then so perfectly certain, Knight Huldbrand, that your first wife is really dead ? It scarcely seems so to me. I will not indeed say anything of the mysterious

condition in which she may be existing, and I know, too, nothing of it with certainty. But she was a pious and faithful wife, that is beyond all doubt ; and for a fortnight past she has stood at my bedside at night in my dreams, wringing her tender hands in anguish, and sighing out : 'Oh, prevent him, good father ! I am still living ! oh, save his life ! save his soul !' I did not understand what this nightly vision signified; when presently your messenger came, and I hurried hither, not to unite, but to separate, what ought not to be joined together. Leave her, Huldbrand ! Leave him, Bertalda ! He yet belongs to another ; and do you not see grief for his lost wife still written on his pale cheek ? No bridegroom looks thus, and a voice tells me that if you do not leave him, you will never be happy."

The three listeners felt in their innermost heart that Father Heilmann spoke the truth, but they would not believe it. Even the old fisherman was now so infatuated, that he thought it could not be otherwise than they had settled it in their discussions during the last few days. They therefore all opposed the warnings of the priest with a wild and gloomy rashness, until at length the holy father quitted the castle with a sad heart, refusing to accept even for a single night the shelter offered, or to enjoy the refreshments brought him. Huldbrand, however, persuaded himself that the priest was full of whims and fancies, and with dawn of day he sent for a father from the nearest monastery, who, without hesitation, promised to perform the ceremony in a few days.

THE
KNIGHTS' DREAM

CHAPTER XVII

THE KNIGHT'S DREAM

T was between night and dawn of day that the knight was lying on his couch, half waking, half sleeping. Whenever he was on the point of falling asleep, a terror seemed to come upon him and scare his rest away, for his slumbers were haunted with spectres. If he tried, however, to rouse himself in good earnest, he felt fanned as by the wings of a swan, and he heard the soft murmuring of waters, until, soothed by the agreeable delusion, he sank back again into a half-conscious state. At length, he must have fallen sound asleep, for it seemed to him as if he were lifted up upon the fluttering wings of the swans, and borne by them far over land and sea, while they sang to him their sweetest music. "The music of the swan! the music of the swan!" he kept saying to himself; "does it not always portend death?" But it had yet another meaning. All at once he felt as if he were hovering over the Mediterranean Sea. A swan was singing musically in his ear that this was the Mediterranean Sea. And whilst he was looking down upon the waters below, they became clear as crystal, so that he could see through them to the bottom. He was delighted at this, for he could see Undine sitting beneath the crystal arch. It is true she was weeping bitterly, and looking much sadder than in the happy days when they had lived together at the castle of Ringstetten, especially at their commencement, and afterwards also, shortly before they had begun their unhappy Danube excursion. The knight could not help thinking upon all this very fully and deeply, but it did not seem as if Undine perceived him. Meanwhile Kühleborn had approached her, and was on the point of reproving her for her weeping. But she drew herself up, and looked at him with such a noble and commanding air that he almost shrunk back with fear. "Although I live here beneath the waters," said she, "I have yet brought down my soul with me; and therefore I may well weep, although you cannot divine what such tears are. They too are blessed, for everything is blessed to him in whom a true soul dwells." He shook his head incredulously, and said, after some reflection: "And yet, niece, you are subject to the laws of our element, and if he marries again and

186

is unfaithful to you, you are in duty bound to take away his life." "He is a widower to this very hour," replied Undine, "and his sad heart still holds me dear." "He is, however, at the same time betrothed," laughed Kühleborn, with scorn; "and let only a few days pass, and the priest will have given the nuptial blessing, and then you will have to go upon earth to accomplish the death of him who has taken another to wife." "That I cannot do," laughed Undine in return; "I have sealed up the fountain securely against myself and my race." "But suppose he should leave his castle," said Kühleborn, "or should have the fountain opened again! for he thinks little enough of these things." "It is just for that reason," said Undine, still smiling amid her tears, "it is just for that reason that he is now hovering in spirit over the Mediterranean Sea, and is dreaming of this conversation of ours as a warning. I have intentionally arranged it so." Kühleborn, furious with rage, looked up at the knight, threatened, stamped with his feet, and then swift as an arrow shot under the waves. It seemed as if he were swelling in his fury to the size of a whale. Again the swans began to sing, to flap their wings and to fly. It seemed to the knight as if he were soaring away over mountains and streams, and that he at length reached the castle Ringstetten and awoke on his couch.

He did in reality awake upon his couch, and his squire coming in at that moment informed him that Father Heilmann was still lingering in the neighbourhood; that he had met him the night before in the forest, in a hut which he had formed for himself of the branches of trees, and covered with moss and brushwood. To the question what he was doing here, since he would not give the nuptial blessing, he had answered : " There are other blessings besides those at the nuptial altar, and though I have not gone to the wedding, it may be that I shall be at another solemn ceremony. We must be ready for all things. Besides, marrying and mourning are not so unlike, and every one not wilfully blinded must see that well."

The knight placed various strange constructions upon these words, and upon his dream, but it is very difficult to break off a thing which a man has once regarded as certain, and so everything remained as it had been arranged.

HOW THE KNIGHT HULDBRAND IS MARRIED

CHAPTER XVIII

HOW THE KNIGHT HULDBRAND IS MARRIED

F I were to tell you how the marriage-feast passed at castle Ringstetten, it would seem to you as if you saw a heap of bright and pleasant things, but a gloomy veil of mourning spread over them all, the dark hue of which would make the splendour of the whole look less like happiness than a mockery of the emptiness of all earthly joys. It was not that any spectral apparitions disturbed the festive company, for we know that the castle had been secured from the mischief of the threatening water-spirits. But the knight and the fisherman and all the guests felt as if the chief personage were still lacking at

193   o

the feast, and that this chief personage could be none
other than the loved and gentle Undine. Whenever
a door opened, the eyes of all were involuntarily turned
in that direction, and if it was nothing but the butler
with new dishes, or the cup-bearer with a flask of
still richer wine, they would look down again sadly,
and the flashes of wit and merriment which had
passed to and fro, would be extinguished by sad remembrances. The bride was the most thoughtless
of all, and therefore the most happy ; but even to
her it sometimes seemed strange that she should be
sitting at the head of the table, wearing a green
wreath and gold-embroidered attire, while Undine was
lying at the bottom of the Danube, a cold and stiff
corpse, or floating away with the current into the
mighty ocean. For, ever since her father had spoken
of something of the sort, his words were ever ringing
in her ear, and this day especially they were not
inclined to give place to other thoughts.

The company dispersed early in the evening, not
broken up by the bridegroom himself, but sadly
and gloomily by the joyless mood of the guests and
their forebodings of evil. Bertalda retired with her
maidens, and the knight with his attendants ; but at
this mournful festival there was no gay laughing
train of bridesmaids and bridesmen.

Bertalda wished to arouse more cheerful thoughts ;
she ordered a splendid ornament of jewels which
Huldbrand had given her, together with rich apparel
and veils, to be spread out before her, in order that
from these latter she might select the brightest and
most beautiful for her morning attire. Her

attendants were delighted at the opportunity of expressing their good wishes to their young mistress, not failing at the same time to extol the beauty of the bride in the most lively terms. They were more and more absorbed in these considerations, till Bertalda at length, looking in a mirror, said with a sigh : " Ah, but don't you see plainly how freckled I am growing here at the side of my neck ? " They looked at her throat, and found the freckles as their fair mistress had said, but they called them beauty-spots, and mere tiny blemishes only tending to enhance the whiteness of her delicate skin. Bertalda shook her head and asserted that a spot was always a defect. " And I could remove them," she sighed at last, " only the fountain is closed from which I used to have that precious and purifying water. Oh! if I had but a flask of it to-day ! " " Is that all ? " said an alert waiting-maid, laughing, as she slipped from the apartment. " She will not be so mad," exclaimed Bertalda, in a pleased and surprised tone, " she will not be so mad as to have the stone removed from the fountain, this very evening ? " At the same moment they heard the men crossing the court-yard, and could see from the window how the officious waiting-woman was leading them straight up to the fountain, and that they were carrying levers and other instruments on their shoulders. " It is certainly my will," said Bertalda, smiling, " if only it does not take too long." And, happy in the sense that a look from her now was able to effect what had formerly been so painfully refused her, she watched the progress of the work in the moonlit castle-court.

The men raised the enormous stone with an effort ; now and then indeed one of their number would sigh, as he remembered that they were destroying the work of their former beloved mistress. But the labour was far lighter than they had imagined. It seemed as if a power within the spring itself were aiding them in raising the stone. " It is just," said the workmen to each other in astonishment, " as if the water within had become a springing fountain." And the stone rose higher and higher, and almost without the assistance of the workmen, it rolled slowly down upon the pavement with a hollow sound. But from the opening of the fountain there rose solemnly a white column of water ; at first they imagined it had really become a springing fountain, till they perceived that the rising form was a pale female figure veiled in white. She was weeping bitterly, raising her hands wailingly above her head and ringing them, as she walked with a slow and serious step to the castle-building. The servants fled from the spring ; the bride, pale and stiff with horror, stood at the window with her attendants. When the figure had now come close beneath her room, it looked moaningly up to her, and Bertalda thought she could recognize beneath the veil the pale features of Undine. But the sorrowing form passed on, sad, reluctant, and faltering, as if passing to execution.

Bertalda screamed out that the knight was to be called, but none of her maids ventured from the spot ; and even the bride herself became mute, as if trembling at her own voice.

While they were still standing fearfully at the

window, motionless as statues, the strange wanderer
had reached the castle, had passed up the well-known
stairs, and through the well-known halls, ever in
silent tears. Alas! how differently had she once
wandered through them!

The knight, partly undressed, had already dismissed his attendants, and in a mood of deep
dejection he was standing before a large mirror; a
taper was burning dimly beside him. There was a
gentle tap at his door. Undine used to tap thus
when she wanted playfully to tease him. "It is all
fancy," said he to himself; "I must seek my nuptial
bed." "So you must, but it must be a cold one!"
he heard a tearful voice say from without, and then
he saw in the mirror his door opening slowly—slowly
—and the white figure entered, carefully closing it
behind her. "They have opened the spring," said
she softly, "and now I am here, and you must die."
He felt in his paralyzed heart that it could not be
otherwise, but covering his eyes with his hands he
said: "Do not make me mad with terror in my
hour of death. If you wear a hideous face behind
that veil, do not raise it, but take my life, and let me
see you not." "Alas!" replied the figure, "will you
then not look upon me once more? I am as fair as
when you wooed me on the promontory." "Oh, if
it were so!" sighed Huldbrand, "and if I might die
in your fond embrace!" "Most gladly, my loved
one," said she; and throwing her veil back, her lovely
face smiled forth divinely beautiful. Trembling
with love and with the approach of death, she kissed
him with a holy kiss; but not relaxing her hold she

pressed him fervently to her, and wept as if she would weep away her soul. Tears rushed into the knight's eyes, and seemed to surge through his heaving breast, till at length his breathing ceased, and he fell softly back from the beautiful arms of Undine, upon the pillows of his couch—a corpse.

"I have wept him to death," said she to some servants who met her in the antechamber ; and, passing through the affrighted group, she went slowly out towards the fountain.

LESS LIKE   HAPPINESS
THAN A HOLLOW MOCKERY OF THE
EMPTINESS OF ALL EARTHLY JOYS.

1897

CHAPTER XIX

How the Knight Huldbrand was buried

FATHER HEILMANN had returned to the castle as soon as the death of the lord of Ringstetten had been made known in the neighbourhood, and he appeared at the very same moment that the monk who had married the unfortunate couple was fleeing from the gates overwhelmed with fear and terror. "It is well," replied Heilmann, when he was informed of this ; "now my duties begin, and I need no associate." Upon this he began to console the bride, now a widow, small result as it produced upon her worldly thoughtless mind. The old fisherman, on the other hand, although heartily grieved, was far more resigned to the fate which had befallen his daughter and son-in-law, and while Bertalda could not refrain from abusing Undine as a murderess and sorceress, the old man calmly said : "It could not be otherwise after all ; I see nothing in it but the judgment of God, and no one's heart has been more deeply grieved by Huldbrand's death than that of her by whom it was inflicted—the poor forsaken Undine !"

At the same time he assisted in arranging the funeral solemnities as befitted the rank of the deceased.

The knight was to be interred in a village churchyard which was filled with the graves of his ancestors. And this church had been endowed with rich privileges and gifts both by these ancestors and by himself. His shield and helmet lay already on the coffin, to be lowered with it into the grave, for Sir Huldbrand of Ringstetten had died the last of his race ; the mourners began their sorrowful march, singing requiems under the bright calm canopy of heaven ; Father Heilmann walked in advance, bearing a high crucifix, and the inconsolable Bertalda followed, supported by her aged father. Suddenly, in the midst of the black-robed attendants in the widow's train, a snow-white figure was seen, closely veiled, and wringing her hands with fervent sorrow. Those near whom she moved felt a secret dread, and retreated either backwards or to the side, increasing by their movements the alarm of the others near to whom the white stranger was now advancing, and thus a confusion in the funeral-train was well-nigh beginning. Some of the military escort were so daring as to address the figure, and to attempt to remove it from the procession ; but she seemed to vanish from under their hands, and yet was immediately seen advancing again amid the dismal cortége with slow and solemn step. At length, in consequence of the continued shrinking of the attendants to the right and to the left, she came close behind Bertalda. The figure now moved so slowly that the widow did not perceive it, and it walked meekly and humbly behind her undisturbed.

This lasted till they came to the churchyard,

where the procession formed a circle round the open grave. Then Bertalda saw her unbidden companion, and starting up half in anger and half in terror, she commanded her to leave the knight's last resting-place. The veiled figure, however, gently shook her head in refusal, and raised her hands as if in humble supplication to Bertalda, deeply agitating her by the action, and recalling to her with tears how Undine had so kindly wished to give her that coral necklace on the Danube. Father Heilmann motioned with his hand and commanded silence, as they were to pray in mute devotion over the body, which they were now covering with the earth. Bertalda knelt silently, and all knelt, even the gravediggers among the rest, when they had finished their task. But when they rose again, the white stranger had vanished ; on the spot where she had knelt there gushed out of the turf a little silver spring, which rippled and murmured away till it had almost entirely encircled the knight's grave ; then it ran further and emptied itself into a lake which lay by the side of the burial-place. Even to this day the inhabitants of the village show the spring ; and cherish the belief that it is the poor rejected Undine, who in this manner still embraces her husband in her loving arms.

Other fantasy titles from Dedalus include:

The Arabian Nightmare – Robert Irwin   £5.95 (hardback)
The Revenants – Geoffrey Farrington   £3.95
The Illumination of Alice J. Cunningham – Lyn Webster   £5.95
Mr Narrator – Pat Gray   £4.95
The Golem – Gustav Meyrink   £4.95
La-Bas – J. K. Huysmans   £4.95
The Cathedral – J. K. Huysmans   £6.95
Les Diaboliques – Barbey D'Aurevilly   £4.95
Baron Munchausen – Erich Raspe   £4.95
The Red Laugh – Leonid Andreyev   £4.95
The Little Angel – Leonid Andreyev   £4.95

Forthcoming titles include:

The Acts of the Apostates – Geoffrey Farrington   £6.95
The Memoirs of the Year 2500 – Louis-Sebastian Mercier   £6.95
Seraphita – Balzac   £4.95
Micromegas – Voltaire   £4.95